The Stories of David Bergelson

Judaic Traditions in Literature, Music, and Art
Ken Frieden and Harold Bloom, Series Editors

The Stories of
David Bergelson

YIDDISH SHORT FICTION FROM RUSSIA

. . .

Translated and with an Introduction by

GOLDA WERMAN

Foreword by Aharon Appelfeld

Syracuse University Press

First Edition 1996
96 97 98 99 00 01   6 5 4 3 2 1

Permission granted by Lev Bergelson to publish translations of David Bergelson's stories is gratefully acknowledged.

The paper used in this publication meets the minimum requirements of American National Standard for Information Sciences—Permanence of Paper for Printed Library Materials, ANSI Z39.48-1984. ∞™

Library of Congress Cataloging-in-Publication Data
Bergelson, David, 1884–1952.
[Short stories. English. Selections]
The stories of David Bergelson : Yiddish short fiction from Russia / translated and with an introduction by Golda Werman ; with a foreword by Aharon Appelfeld.
p.   cm.—(Jewish traditions in literature, music, and art)
Includes bibliographical references.
ISBN 0-8156-0402-5 (paperback : alk. paper).—ISBN 0-8156-2712-2 (cloth : alk. paper)
1. Bergelson, David, 1884–1952—Translations into English.
I. Werman, Golda, 1930—   . II. Title. III. Series.
PJ5129.B45A23   1996
839'.0933—dc20   96-17952

Manufactured in the United States of America

To Bob, always,
and to the memory of our parents,
Chaim Isaac and Breindel Spiera,
Moshe Gershon and Rashe Werman

David Bergelson, the most innovative stylist in modern Yiddish literature, was born on August 12, 1884, in the Ukraine. Unlike his predecessors he wrote for a sophisticated Yiddish audience, among whom he quickly became a favorite. Readers of English do not know him because very few of his stories have previously been translated. Bergelson was murdered by Stalin on his sixty-eighth birthday for the crime of writing in Yiddish. Many other Yiddish writers were killed along with him.

Golda Werman was born in Germany, grew up in the United States, and lives in Jerusalem with her husband and family. Her most recent publication is *Milton and Midrash,* a study of the midrashic sources of *Paradise Lost.* She has translated many Yiddish works into English.

Contents

David Bergelson / *frontispiece*

Foreword, Aharon Appelfeld / *ix*

Acknowledgments / *xi*

Introduction / *xiii*

Remnants / *1*

Impoverished / *14*

Departing / *25*

Bibliography / *155*

Foreword

Aharon Appelfeld

David Bergelson is the most important Yiddish writer, following the three classical authors who established modern Yiddish literature: Mendele Mocher Sforim, I. L. Peretz, and Sholem Aleichem. His belief in communism, his voluntary return to Russia, and his subservience to the literary dictates of the Revolution eventually flawed his later writings. Despite this, the totality of his creative output has withstood the test of time, especially the works he wrote before his enslavement to communism.

The reader interested in learning about the transition from the typical-general to the personal-individual in Yiddish literature will do well to turn to the stories of Bergelson. In them there is an entire universe waiting to be uncovered. Bergelson paved new roads in Yiddish literature and brought it into the modern age.

A small sample of Bergelson's writings has previously been translated into English, but these translations cannot be compared to what the translator Golda Werman has now done. Ms. Werman has selected the richest and the most complex of Bergelson's Yiddish stories and has rendered them into their literary equivalents in English. She presents us with a highly readable text that is sensitive and vital, not a halting translation but a creative work in its own right.

Acknowledgments

I wish to extend my gratitude to Abraham Nowersztern for first introducing me to the works of David Bergelson and for suggesting that I translate the novella *Departing,* to Seth Wolitz for sharing his love of the story "Remnants" with me, and to my students' enthusiastic reading of these texts and their often surprising insights.

Introduction

On a mild December evening in Jerusalem in 1993, I attended a memorial meeting for the Yiddish writers and other artists who were murdered by Stalin after World War II. The event was very well attended; every seat in the library of the Russian Immigrant Society's Zionist Forum was occupied, and many people stood in the aisles and at the back of the crowded, overheated room, fanning themselves with envelopes, handkerchiefs, anything that came to hand. The Russians had not forgotten their brothers who were murdered during the dark days of Stalin's reign for the crime of keeping Yiddish culture alive.

The invited speakers sat in a semicircle at the front of the hall, facing the audience. Above them hung a portrait of Solomon Mikhoels, the famous actor and director of the Moscow State Yiddish Theater and leader of the Jewish community; he was killed in 1948 in a staged automobile accident, a favorite means of execution by the KGB. On a shelf at the far side of the reading room, a large photo of David Bergelson, the foremost modern Yiddish stylist, looked down on his Russian compatriots. He was imprisoned in 1948, under gruesome conditions, and was never heard from again. His family was not allowed to visit him or to send him letters. They were merely informed that he was shot on August 12,

1952, which was his sixty-eighth birthday. Many other Yiddish writers were executed on the same day.

Bergelson's son, Lev Bergelson, sat at the center of the semicircle. A famous chemist, he had recently immigrated to Israel from Moscow, where he was a member of the Russian Academy of Science, an almost unheard of honor for a Jew. Now he is a professor at the Hadassah Medical School in Jerusalem and at the National Institutes of Health in Bethesda, Maryland. At his left sat Natalia Mikhoels, Solomon Mikhoels's daughter; she and her sister immigrated to Israel in the seventies after years of struggle with the Soviet authorities for an exit visa. At Lev Bergelson's right was the violinist Lavia Hofstein, daughter of the renowned Yiddish poet David Hofstein, who was shot on the same fateful day as David Bergelson, and for the same crime of writing in Yiddish. His widow, Feyge, was too ill to attend the ceremony, but people remembered her fondly. In the seventies, soon after settling in Tel Aviv, she wrote a lovely Yiddish memoir about her life with the poet, their good years together and their suffering under Stalin.

Seated next to Lavia was the son of the Yiddish lyric poet Shmuel Halkin, whose poems of yearning for Zion so outraged the communist authorities that he was forced to recant publicly. This ended his career as a poet, and he switched to the safer profession of translating classical writers—Shakespeare, Gorki, and Pushkin—into Yiddish. Despite his discretion, Halkin was arrested in 1948 and sent to a remote area of Siberia where conditions were very harsh; in 1955, desperately ill and broken in spirit, he was allowed to return home for medical treatment. He died a few years later.

Two buxom, middle-aged women sat next to each other at Natalia's left: one, a former Yiddish actress, had been trained by the great Mikhoels himself; the other, a librarian, was in the process of cataloging the archives of Mikhoels's Yiddish Theater.

The program began with a girls' choir singing a medley of Yiddish songs, followed by the actress reading one of Hofstein's Yiddish poems. And that ended the sound of Yiddish for the evening—no one else uttered a Yiddish word. The master of ceremonies introduced the speakers in Russian, the speakers addressed the audience in Russian, all the announcements were in Russian, and all the questions from the audience were in Russian. Yiddish, it seems, was reserved for ceremonial rites: little girls crooning *tumba-la-laika* and aging actresses declaiming Yiddish verse, nostalgic concessions to a remembered past. Serious discourse, however, requires a living language, and the speakers no longer thought and functioned in Yiddish—not even those who grew up in Yiddish-speaking homes, in families that were dedicated to Yiddish culture.

It is estimated that before World War II eleven million people throughout the world spoke Yiddish, and many read Yiddish literature. Publishing houses printed Yiddish books for every age and on every subject, the Yiddish theater flourished, popular Yiddish movies were produced, and Yiddish newspapers provided their readers with poetry, essays, stories, even novels in serialized form. And these were endlessly discussed—in the streets, at home, and in the coffeehouses. Today, the Yiddish language is tottering at the edge of death, despite some efforts to revive it, and the number of its speakers can be counted in the thousands rather than in millions. Poland, the former center of Yiddish culture, no longer has Jews. Russia's Yiddish was essentially wiped out by Stalin. The Jews of the West lost Yiddish somewhere on the road to their brilliant acculturation, and all that remains is nostalgia. Yiddish literature is now rarely read in the original.

David Bergelson (1884–1952) is therefore all but unknown to those who do not read Yiddish, for only a few of his writings—some short stories and a novel—have been translated into English. Yiddishists consider him the successor to the three classic modern Yiddish authors—Mendele Mocher Sforim, Sholem Aleichem, and I. L. Peretz—but, unlike them, Bergelson wrote for a cultured, highly educated audience, not for the masses.

His great predecessors had forged a literature out of their lives and dreams, when life was simpler, the lines more clearly drawn. Their world was the shtetl, and they knew it intimately; they were connected to its institutions, understood the people, recognized the enemy. By Bergelson's time the world had changed. The Revolution of 1905, which raised people's hopes for a better life, created an exodus to the industrialized cities and to America, and the shtetl inevitably declined. Of those who remained, in that heady period between the two socialist revolutions, many no longer accepted the values and traditions that had served their parents and grandparents so well. They did not want their lives anchored to the synagogue and to the study house.

Yet they had not managed to create better lives for themselves. The freedom to doubt, they soon learned, created more problems than it solved, and the newly open social structure was not so easy to penetrate. They were not yet attuned to the world of industry and competition, and the coldness and indifference of the big city frightened them. The individual who had once been part of a community, connected to its institutions and committed to its values, was now alone and experienced the angst and pain of alienation from society. Bergelson captures the dreariness of the uncommitted life and portrays characters who suffer from ennui and depression as a result of the loosening ties to the shtetl and to religion.

Bergelson's view is not narrow, however, and his focus is not solely on Jewish concerns. Although his setting is the declining shtetl, his theme is the suffering of lonely, alienated people everywhere. His characters suffer from the same malaise that afflicts the many alienated in our own inhospitable world. Bergelson is more interested in psychology than in theology. Suicide, as he describes it, is an emotional tragedy, a tragedy of the human condition, not a sin.

Bergelson is particularly impressive in his sensitive psychological probing of women, more vulnerable now in their new roles and with their increased freedom. In a style that is both lyrical and precise, using rhythmic repetitions and innovative dialogue but never an extra word or syllable, Bergelson uncovers the woman's soul and reveals her basic nature—the tenderness as well as the determination. And always there is a heavy atmosphere of gloom and oppression over her, the gloom of the dying shtetl.

He had learned much from the Russians. To depict the new world of the declining shtetl and the disaffected in that society, Bergelson had to free himself from the forms and themes of the Yiddish writers who preceded him. In the process of liberating himself from the anxiety of influence, he created a style that is unique, innovative, and original. He used the language of the old Yiddish writers, molded to suit his more worldly and contemporary concerns; and he followed the Russian writers—Tolstoy, Turgenev, Dostoyevsky, Gorki, Andreyev—in creating characters with emotional depth. From Chekhov he learned about mood and atmosphere

The style, however, is his own. Bergelson uses echoes and patterns of repetition as lyrical devices to elicit the reader's emotional response; he makes use of internal dialogue to reveal the thoughts behind the words of his heroes; and he analyzes the psychological state of his characters to a degree unprecedented in Yiddish literature. He enjoys the small moves, the details of existence, the little twists and turns that make the quotidian interesting. But he is a realist, and therefore his vision of life is essentially tragic.

His shtetl is hazy and there is the dolor of death all around, but it is a real world. His shtetl is not peopled by warm and deeply religious Jews, as in Sholem Aleichem, nor is it a society so filled with poverty and superstition that it invariably chokes its inhabitants, as in Mendele Mocher Sforim. He portrays the Yiddish-speaking intelligentsia after the failed Revolution of 1905 as frightened and confused, often aimless, talking late into the night as a substitute for action. They are no longer religious and no longer feel the pull of the shtetl community, yet they are too unsure of themselves to leave.

David Bergelson was born on August 12, 1884, in Okhrimovo, near Uman in the Ukraine. He was the youngest child in a Hasidic family. His father, a successful wood merchant, died when David was a boy of nine. His mother, a cultured woman who loved Yiddish literature, saw to it that David was tutored in secular subjects, including modern languages, while he attended the local *heder,* the traditional religious boys' school, where he studied Bible, history, and Talmud. When David was fourteen his mother died and he went to live with his older brothers in the big cities of Kiev, Odessa, and Warsaw. He read widely: Hebrew and Russian literature, world literature in translation, Yiddish literature;

and, like every good Jewish-Russian lad, he played the violin.

His earliest writings were in Hebrew and Russian, but he switched to Yiddish in 1907 with his story "The Deaf One" (Der Toyber); thereafter he used Yiddish exclusively. His first novella, *At the Depot* (Arum Vokzal), written in 1908, won him immediate critical acclaim. During the next two years he wrote some of his best stories, including "Remnants" (Droyb) and "Impoverished" (Yordim), both included in this volume. One of his most popular works is the children's book, *Fayvel's Tales* (Fayvel's Mayses), which adults soon adopted as their own. With the publication of his novel, *When All is Said and Done* (Nokh Alemen) in 1913, his reputation as a major Yiddish writer was firmly established; the critics declared him an outstanding talent, original, brilliant, and authentic, and predicted that his innovative style would have an important impact on modern Yiddish letters. During this period he began work on his novella *Departing* (Opgang), also included in this volume. It was not published until 1920. Many other works were published during this early, fertile period, including *Joseph Schur* (1913) and *In a Backwoods Town* (1914). In 1928 the short novel *Civil War* was printed in a collection of stories. A list of Bergelson's works that have been translated into English appears at the end of this book.

Bergelson's early works were written at a time when Yiddish literature flourished in the Soviet Union and Yiddish books sold in the hundreds of thousands. He was optimistic about the future of Yiddish letters but felt that new forms were needed. In an early article entitled "Literature and Society," he declared that there was an organic tie between society and literature, the social forms being the bricks and mortar of a writer's work. The Revolution created a new society that did not fit the old forms, yet there were no new forms to replace them.

To meet the need for fresh styles, Bergelson and other Yiddish writers who were interested in experimenting with new forms founded a literary society in 1912, in Kiev, called *The League for Jewish Culture*. The group included the famous writers Der Nister, Peretz Markish, David Hofstein, and Leib Kvitko, among others. All were grounded in the Jewish sources; but they had studied Russian and European literature, too. Symbolism and Impressionism fascinated them, and they experimented with the techniques of these literary movements in an attempt to divert Yiddish literature away from the traditional forms. One of the group's major accomplishments was the publication of a two-volume miscellany called *Our Own* (Eygns), which appeared between 1918 and 1920 under Bergelson's editorship. It emphasized poetry, but other forms of literature and criticism were also represented.

Yiddish literature continued to thrive in the early years of the Bolshevik government. Between 1917 and 1921 some 850 Yiddish books were printed; many new Yiddish newspapers appeared; literary journals published Yiddish stories, poems, and criticism; and the Yiddish theater reached new heights of excellence under the direction of Solomon Mikhoels. Yiddish writers were supported financially, and there was enough flexibility to allow them to experiment with new styles.

Beginning in the 1920s, however, things began to change. Material shortages caused by the civil war made it difficult for writers to concentrate on creative work. Furthermore, Bolshevik restraints were becoming more and more intolerable as writers were forced to follow the vague dictates of socialist realism. Many Yiddish authors emigrated, among them Kadya Molodovsky, Der Nister, and Leib Kvitko. Bergelson had already left for Berlin in 1921, where he worked for the Yiddish newspaper, the *Forward,* contributing an article or a story each week. But he was restless and traveled widely, settling in Denmark for a time, and in Poland. In the United States he lectured to large audiences in New York, Baltimore, Chicago, Philadelphia, and other cities, reading from his works in progress.

He was very critical of the state of Yiddish culture in the United States. Writers for the popular Yiddish newspapers and for the stage pandered to a poor, mainly uneducated audience. Intellectuals, including the group of poets who called themselves Die Yunge (The Young Ones)—Mani Leib, Reuven Ayzland, Zishe Landau, David Ignatoff, and others—received little remuneration or recognition. They were mainly poor laborers who wrote whenever they could snatch an hour or two from their work. Bergelson identified with their poetic aims; they, too, sought to create a new and vital literature that was not based on the old, folkloristic traditions. But he found their low status and poverty intolerable. In Russia poets were respected—and subsidized.

Over the years Bergelson had become ever more convinced that communism was the only hope for mankind. In keeping with his communist sympathies, he left his job at the *Forward* in 1926 for a position with a lower salary at the communist newspaper *Freiheit,* and he published novels that supported the aims of the revolution. *Measure of Justice* (Midas Hadin), written in 1925, is about an officer in the political police; though a decent enough person in many ways, he has no pangs of conscience when he orders people shot. The killings are not the acts of an individual but part of the historical process. The revolution creates its own justice.

The first volume of *By the Dnieper,* published in 1932, when he was in Germany, has a ten-year-old hero named Penek who despises the bourgeois values of his home and prefers to associate with the servants and the people in the poorer parts of town. He has never respected his father, a Jewish scholar, and he spouts the usual formulas in praise of the communist revolution. The second volume, written after Bergelson returned to the Soviet Union, deals with Penek grown into a revolutionary.

Bergelson returned to Moscow in 1933, convinced that the new social order would encourage Yiddish writers. Indeed, he believed that there would be a great blossoming of Yiddish literature in the Soviet Union. Other equally optimistic Yiddish writers returned with him, including the poets Leib Kvitko and Peretz Markish, the novelist Moshe Kulbak, and the critic Max Erik. On the way to Moscow, Bergelson visited the autonomous Jewish area of Birobidzhan, where Yiddish was to have been the official language; he wrote *Birobidzhan Stories* after this visit.

Jewish writers did flourish in Moscow, but very briefly. Mikhoels's Yiddish Theater, which had reached the highest standards of art and had made a major contribution to Russian culture, was a great source of pride for the Jews. Yiddish writers were supported with generous royalties and given good housing. However, very quickly things changed. Moshe Litvakov, a fanatically loyal communist who was the editor-in-chief of the leading Yiddish newspaper, *Truth* (Der Emes), was arrested. Moishe Kulbak and Itze Kharik, both famous Yiddish writers, were imprisoned; Kharik was executed, and Kulbak died in a slave labor camp in 1940. Other Yiddish writers were sent to concentration camps or tortured in prison.

The atmosphere was unbearable for Yiddish writers. They were treated with the greatest suspicion; every word they wrote was censored. The strictures of socialist realism were so vague that anything Jews wrote could be considered illegitimate, depending on the mood or the prejudices of the examiner. According to the doctrine of socialist realism, art belonged to the people and had to be intelligible even to the least educated. Because the function of literature was to depict truth, and because the communist party was the source of all truth, only the writer who adhered closely to the party line was a true representative of art. No individual expression was possible in this system, nor was an opinion that differed from the party line or a view of life that might raise questions or doubts in the reader.

To further squelch Yiddish writers, a new term of opprobrium was invented: "cosmopolitanism." Because Russian culture was supposedly undermined by the Jewish content in Yiddish writings, Yiddish works were censored more and more scrupulously for Jewish content. Anything that touched on Jewish culture and the Jewish past was considered separatist and nationalistic, even including folklore or jokes. All Hebrew had to be excised from the Yiddish language, and every trace of religion, including all references to the Bible, had to be removed from Yiddish works. Such strictures not only left the language dull and colorless but also stopped up major sources of inspiration for Yiddish writers.

With these severe restrictions Bergelson could not even consider returning to his innovative experiments. If he wanted to write at all, he had to write politically correct books, not stories about his own experiences. As a result, the quality of his writing declined seriously; he could not abide by the strictures of socialist realism, vague as they were, and continue to write delicate, lyrical stories that explored the motives and responses of the individual. In the process of writing propaganda and pandering to the communist censors, his style became unrefined, even coarse.

None of the returning writers had foreseen the black future that awaited Yiddish in the Soviet Union. Stalin exterminated half a million Jews and shut down all Jewish cultural institutions, including 750 schools that taught Yiddish. It was obvious that the Yiddish language would meet the same fate as Hebrew and be annihilated root and branch.

When the Germans invaded Russia, Bergelson's dormant Jewish feelings could no longer be contained. He wrote a play, *Prince Reuveni,* in which he talks about the ancient dream of a Jewish homeland, using the Inquisition as a barely disguised metaphor for life in the Soviet Union. This was a daring move. Other Yiddish writers were similarly brought back to their Jewish roots, even including the fanatic communist Itzik Fefer and the poet Peretz Markish, who had written paeans of praise to Stalin.

The year 1948 was horrendous for Jewish artists. Isaac Babel, who wrote in Russian, was executed. Mikhoels was murdered, and his theater was closed a year later. Bergelson and other Yiddish writers were arrested, as were almost all the intellectuals who had served Stalin on the Jewish Anti-Fascist Committee. By 1952 most of the Yiddishists had been killed, and even simple Jews were so frightened that they destroyed their own Yiddish books.

·   ·   ·

The stories in this volume of Bergelson's writings all belong to his early period, when he believed in the integrity of the artist and expressed himself freely, unbound by socialist realism. They reveal Bergelson as a penetrating psychologist who feels the pain of his characters, victims of the human condition who are undermined by fate. His profound understanding of human nature is set off by the lyrical qualities of his prose style, exemplary for his time and still cogent and compelling today. In order to demonstrate these qualities I have chosen the stories "Remnants" and "Impoverished" and the novella *Departing.*

"Remnants" is the story of an orphaned servant, Beyla Henya, who is born to every disadvantage that a young woman in the shtetl can have. She is not only poor but also profoundly ugly, with deep pockmarks and crossed eyes. To disguise her physical deformities she covers her face with a white kerchief, and to endure the pain of her difficult existence she develops pride—and hope. In a triumph of the human spirit, she forcefully reorganizes her perceptual field and refuses to see her situation for what it is; instead, she dreams of marrying a respectable man one day. She never speaks.

In Beyla Henya, Bergelson has created the modern feminist ideal: a strong-willed, stubborn, spunky woman who knows what she wants and is not afraid to reach for it. She will not submit to her husband in a loveless marriage. She does not let the harsh circumstances of her life destroy her. And she stubbornly clings to her dream until it comes true; she finally marries a respectable man who is as silent as she is.

Bergelson's point of view is modern enough to please the most fastidious feminist critic, yet the story was written at the turn of the century and concerns the lives of simple, unsophisticated people living in a shtetl. Bergelson gives the characters a realistic, visual presence by using concise, tren-

chant details: Beyla Henya's rich relative wears a black worsted shawl; the husband's sister wears a peasant's kerchief;
Beyla Henya and her husband eat out of the same dish; a man
urinates in the street, his coat covered with the whitewash he
has just brushed against. And lest the fairy-tale ending seem
far-fetched, Bergelson emends it with an ironic twist that
qualifies the happy outcome and makes the narrative wholly
plausible.

"Impoverished" is a story about two unmarried sisters,
Zivia and Rochl, who live with their blind father in a decaying house that smells of mold and death. The house is unsta-
ble, sinking ever deeper into the ground, a metaphor for the
family's grave-like existence. Poverty has brought the sisters
low—psychologically, socially, and spiritually. They are
helplessly locked into their fate.

The father lies on the couch all day, bored to death,
dreaming of the old days when he was rich. Rochl, the older
sister, has given up on life. Zivia is depressed, but she has
occasional bursts of energy when she cleans the house from
top to bottom, desperately trying to fight her own death by
bringing the house to life again. Shmiel, the successful
brother, never visits.

And there is silence. Zivia never speaks at all during her
bouts of depression; she can't even bear to be spoken to. The
sisters don't have anything to say to each other because nothing ever happens to them. The old man mumbles into his
beard, and when he talks too much, his daughters silence
him. The wealthy brother has no interest at all in communi-
cating with his family.

How, one might ask, can a story built on words portray
silence? Eschewing the dramatist's footnote, "there was silence," Bergelson's artistry allows him to illustrate the silence

in the fabric of his descriptions. The reader senses the silence,
is weighed down and oppressed by it. To see and feel how
Bergelson handles silence is sufficient reason to read the
stories.

It is telling to compare Bergelson's use of silence in the
two stories. In "Remnants" the silence is innocent and un-
affected. The old teacher has almost forgotten how to speak
since his wife died. He would like to talk to Beyla Henya
after their marriage but can't because he doesn't know her
name; and Beyla Henya can't overcome her shyness to speak
to him. The silence between them is gentle, suggesting sym-
pathy and even love. We sense silence here as understanding,
a form of communication. When the old teacher finally
breaks his silence to praise Beyla Henya's cooking, "a delicious dish, a wonderful pumpkin," she experiences the greatest happiness she has ever known. She continues to maintain
her silence, however, until he dies. Then she finally gives
voice to her feelings and cries out, "You liked pumpkin . . .
so I made you pumpkin."

The silence in "Impoverished" is not the innocent silence
of "Remnants." It is oppressive and harsh—a mark of Zivia's
depression, of Shmiel's indifference, and of the sisters' cruelty
to their father. The sisters speak mainly to themselves, crying
out in their bitterness. "Dear God in Heaven, what does Zivia
want from my life?" Rochl cries helplessly. "God in Heaven,
we're rotting here before we're even in our shrouds," wails
Zivia. This is not communication, nor is it intended to be.
The father sighs and mumbles to himself, "Oh, dear God and
Father, King of the Universe," but no one listens; he might
as well be silent. Shmiel, the rich son, remains distant and
silent, never so much as adding a note to the check he sends
each month to his father and sisters. When his train passes

through the shtetl, Shmiel has nothing to say; he merely extends his gloved hand out of the window and touches his father lightly.

In the novella *Departing,* we are quickly made to understand that life is suffused with pain and can have no meaning. Once we accept these givens, Bergelson asks, "Is suicide a legitimate solution to the hurt and a remedy for the vacuum?" Suicide, as a theme, had been taboo in Yiddish literature. Bergelson, the first to deal with the subject, acted on his belief that every aspect of life was proper material for an author. He fashioned a highly innovative and artistic novella, full of surprising dialogues with the dead man, along with romance and love. Bergelson understands suicide as stemming from psychological poverty and a lack of values rather than from hunger and physical pain.

Melech, a gifted and charming young man, dies suddenly, and his friend Chaim Moshe, a teacher of mathematics, comes to the shtetl to investigate the cause. During his careful and painstaking search, Chaim Moshe discovers that Melech took poison. Chaim Moshe carries on a continuous debate with himself and with the dead Melech on the question of suicide: is it an acceptable solution to a life devoid of meaning?

The background of the novella is the dying shtetl and the dissolution of values: "Clouds chase each other across the blue sky and their shadows below play the same game in the street and in the marketplace. But in heaven everything is pure gold; below the imitation is tainted and unclean." One of the characters, Esther Fich, a student who returns reluctantly to the shtetl every summer, puts it succinctly, "Nobody ever dies here—they just fade away." The void left by the breakup of the old, established way of life, by the weakening of a religion-based life-style that gave meaning to community, is not easily filled, even by economic success. The big city, to which Chaim Moshe and his friend Melech had turned for a life of excitement and promise, failed to satisfy the young men. It is too impersonal, too empty and devoid of meaning.

Bergelson presents a wide variety of shtetl characters, among whom the women are the most memorable. One of them is Ethel Kadis, whose engagement to Melech gave her a reason to live. His death leaves her with "the look of a woman who knows deep down that life is mocking her, but . . . pretends indifference." Another is Chava Poyzner, whose solution to an empty life is to marry rich and leave the dying shtetl. The most sympathetic of the women is Channeke Loyber, who tenderly cares for her little motherless brother and whose love for Chaim Moshe ultimately saves him from suicide.

The men include Praeger, the principal of the local school, who has nothing but loathing for all the respectable people in the shtetl. Although a highly educated and successful teacher, he is spiteful and vindictive, spewing out his anger on anyone he feels is above him in status. To forget his problems he drinks, mainly with low-life characters. And there is Dr. Grabay, a former communist party orator who now stacks away his money. He has not much else to live for; his wife has left him and their little daughter for another man.

Chaim Moshe, who returns to the shtetl to find out why Melech died so suddenly, is a modern intellectual—precise, logical, and unbendingly hard on himself. In his debates with himself and with the imagined, reincarnated Melech, Chaim Moshe accuses his friend of giving in to the world. They had both agreed to live by the principle of "the silent protest." But Melech was not satisfied; he wanted happiness. His act of suicide is a betrayal, according to Chaim Moshe, who claims to have no illusions about life.

The novel begins on a cold, rainy day with Melech's funeral. Chaim Moshe discovers Melech's suicide, decries it— and, coming full circle, contemplates suicide as a solution for his own problems. But he is saved by love. The novel ends as the sun rises to the promise of a beautiful day.

Silence is again a major theme. In the city the two friends would repeat over and over again, "The silent protest, the eternal silent protest." Bergelson does not explain the meaning of the motto; instead he describes the friends as destined to walk the city like strangers, seeing and hearing everything and saying nothing. Melech has impressed everyone with his shy smile and his silence, and people loved him. They believed that his silence indicated great wisdom and knowledge. But, in fact, he fooled them all, committing suicide under their noses with small doses of poison while making them all believe that he was ill.

Not even silence can be trusted, Bergelson tells us—not in so many words, rather through the plot and the characters. And the other side of the scale is balanced with our realization that suicide, successful as a solution or not, is the ultimate silence. Man, Chaim Moshe tells us, dies alone. When his time comes, he *wants* to die alone; his funeral will be at night, and no one will come. Here is his final, silent protest.

But there is another silence, Bergelson informs us, a silence that is louder than speech, that is truer and more trustworthy. Channeke, who loves to talk, becomes increasingly silent as her love for Chaim Moshe grows. She looks into his eyes and feels that he knows everything she knows, that he has always known. And her sad blue eyes speak to Chaim

Moshe's heart more than words do. At the end of the book, when Channeke comes to Chaim Moshe's room just as he is contemplating suicide, she offers him her silent love. It is perfectly understood. Chaim Moshe, the intellectual, falls silent, too, in the face of love. "Oh, Channeke" is all he says, and all that need be said.

We might ask, as Bergelson undoubtedly does, how can a novelist, a wordsmith, deal so successfully with silence. The irony is obvious and charges Bergelson's language with electric sparks. Do words have meaning? Can acting, even suicide, relieve the angst of a dying, aphonic society? Bergelson illuminates the other side of the moon in his treatment of Channecke. She is portrayed as silent and deferential, but with great native intelligence and emotional depth—she knows what she wants. Channeke understands intuitively that Chaim Moshe is contemplating suicide and acts to intercept that plan.

Bergelson's writings challenge the interpretive skills of the reader, just as his artistry plucks sympathetic chords.

.   .   .

A word about the translation. It has been said that every translation of literature produces a new literary work. The translator's attempt to uncover the writer's intended meaning forces her to engage in the tricky art of interpretation, with all its tantalizing—and egoistic—allures. And, in attempting to render some essence of the original language into the new language, the translator is again in peril. Style cannot be transferred from one language to another; at best the translator may come up with an equivalent in the new language that reproduces the sense of the original.

Bergelson depends on poetic effects to establish mood and

meaning: his Yiddish syntax is complex; his language is both rich and precise; and he uses musical devices, including sound patterns and repetition. The problems of capturing the rhythms of the original language in another tongue are legion. When rendered faithfully, these constructions often grind painfully on the English reader's ear. Since my goal was to make Bergelson's work live in English as it does in Yiddish, I had to make compromises. I had to render Bergelson's flowing Yiddish into readable English and, at the same time, keep as close to the essence of Bergelson's work as I could without making the translation sound foreign.

Not the least of my problems was that Bergelson's language is a perfect match for a phenomenon not clearly represented in the experience of readers of English. These works all take place against the background of the dying shtetl, which casts a pall over everything. It is almost impossible to render Bergelson's rhythms and his haunting, elegiac descriptions into English. Yet these are precisely the stylistic devices that create the gloomy atmosphere that Bergelson aimed for, evoking empathy and enabling the reader to see and feel what Bergelson saw and felt. No translation can do justice to the moody, dark atmosphere created by Bergelson and the language he uses to further his aims; there is no strict counterpart in English to the compelling music of Bergelson's Yiddish.

Great works, however, are more easily translated than inferior works. Bergelson helped by handling the interaction of the background and the action very gently, very delicately. At the end the reader says, "That's right, that's the way it is," and puts down the book with a sigh.

The Stories of David Bergelson

Remnants

I

Beyla Henya was ugly and thin as a rail and her long, drawn face was covered with pockmarks. But ever since she was a young girl she had talked about marrying a fine and respectable man one day. She had been a servant in the home of a rich relative before she was married to a man everyone called Moyshe the Tartar. He was a blacksmith. She never wanted him.

This ate him up. A freak like that—and not want him! And he beat her and beat her—but she still didn't want him.

On Simchas Torah, the holiday of the Rejoicing of the Law, he hit her for the last time.

All day long a cold north wind blew through the shtetl and the skies were gray, as if it were about to rain. The men were seated around the rabbi's table, all eyes turned to him and to the newly appointed beadle, Motl the Redhead, who sat at his side. They were drinking brandy and humming the old familiar melodies. The women sat outside, huddled in their coats; they had placed their chairs in a semicircle near the door so that they could watch the men's high-spirited fun and games. All old friends and cut from the same cloth, they enjoyed a good joke now and then when they were together.

On this cheerful holiday they were pitching watermelon seeds at Yonah Beanpole's beard and chanting, "Yonah! Yonah Beanpole, the devil is coming to take you away!"

Yonah Beanpole pretends not to hear them. Placing himself in direct line of the watermelon seeds, he sings a song to the melody of the prayer for rain in a loud cantorial voice:

Bim-bom-bay
My wife has gone away.
The holiday is o'er
And she flew out the door.
Believe me, I don't mind
She's left the cat behind.

Suddenly someone comes dashing into the rabbi's house, breathless from having raced through the shtetl, and announces, "He's beating his wife again!"

"Who?

"Moyshe the Tartar."

"I hope he bursts wide open."

And they all run out of the rabbi's house at once. One man, not aware that his shoulders are covered with a white powder from having brushed against a newly whitewashed wall, makes his way to the side of the house and, grinning as if he is playing a trick on someone, opens his pants and urinates. When he turns around he sees them all watching Moyshe the Tartar chase his wife Beyla Henya. The Tartar is a huge giant of a man with a blacksmith's stained hands; he spends all his working hours repairing broken axles for the local peasants. Beyla Henya is as thin and puny as a plucked chicken.

Everyone knows that ugly Beyla Henya has a small broken mirror with the silver almost rubbed out that she keeps next to her bed so she can look at herself in privacy. Yet even at this moment when she is running for her life she doesn't forget to hide her pockmarked face under a clean white kerchief; and she lowers her crossed eyes in shame, as if she feels guilty about something. Quickly she heads for the big house across the street where she worked before she was married, and everyone watches as they lock the door behind her. "This is it," they say. "It's all over."

II

The house is a mansion—ancient, stately, and magnificent. It has a flat roof, strong whitewashed walls and handsome acacia trees in front of the large, eight-paned windows. The old trees quiver with the slightest breeze and waving to and fro beneath the cloudy autumn skies, they vex all the poor houses around them with the oft-repeated story: "Once a rich man built this house; and the rich man had a son; and the rich man's son died; and they have many guests—the Jewish doctor, the tax collector, and the police commissioner; and the rich man never goes to prayers."

All around it is muddy and wet. The fields, deserted after the harvest, are heaped so high that the piles of hay seem to touch the endless clouds of winter. Silence reigns except for the occasional hum of a pair of birds passing through and disappearing, leaving behind only the ululating sound of a bell—then nothing. Squalid little houses, half-sunk in the mud, can feel the vibrations of an approaching boot. It is Moyshe the Tartar wandering by at midday to while away the time with the shop owners. But they have nothing to say to each other. Weighed down by pain and sorrow, he stands absolutely still, staring blankly at his boots. Finally he blurts out, "The devil take her."

He means the rich relative in the big house. Beyla Henya

has been with her since Simchas Torah and the lady refuses to let her return to him. The message is always the same: If he agrees to divorce Beyla Henya she will give him fifty rubles.

The Tartar is afraid of the rich relative because the tax collector comes there so often, but he goes to the house anyway because he wants to ask his wife to come back to him. They don't let him come inside and make him wait in the hall, like a beggar. He can hear his wife run out of the kitchen and through the house to hide in her mistress's bedroom. Meanwhile the fat nurse with the pushed-in nose and thick lips comes out of one of the warm inner rooms with a baby in her arms. She makes believe that she is there to rock the infant but she really wants to see the man who made Beyla Henya hide in the bedroom. She stares at him with shy black eyes. Finally the mistress of the house appears and lets out a tirade of invective. And does she have a mouth! It's like a vise. The Tartar, feeling wronged, is tongue-tied in her presence and can only mumble bitterly out of the corner of his mouth, "I hope she chokes."

He's sick of it all. He's lost all interest in his smithy. He has no one to talk to at home; she never had children with him, the pockmarked mouse. He has a sour taste in his mouth and a gnawing at the pit of his stomach. Even the weather is bad. "The devil take her!" he thinks, and he makes up his mind to see her one last time—this time to give her a divorce.

The rich relative, wearing a black worsted shawl over her head, accompanies Beyla Henya to the rabbi's house. She keeps her eyes fastened on the Tartar and listens closely to every word he is asked to repeat by the rabbi, shaking her head from time to time like an expert and making sure that she's getting her fifty rubles worth.

The Tartar's sister, wearing a peasant's kerchief and surrounded by a group of women and children, waits in front of the rabbi's house. She lives in the shtetl and earns her living by reading cards for the peasants and making predictions about whether their stolen goods will ever be found.

"May they both be buried alive and die a horrible death!" she cries. "God, listen to me, turn their bowels into a burning volcano—now!" Anyone watching her from a distance and seeing her eyes riveted on the rabbi's house with her lips moving like that might think that she was praying.

Suddenly the door flies open and the bystanders are surprised to see the divorce party run in every direction through the shtetl.

"What is it?"

"Oh, nothing—nothing at all. The Tartar beat Beyla Henya after the divorce. It's the last time."

III

The Tartar sold his smithy and left the shtetl—but nobody knows where he is. Summer has come and he still hasn't returned. Beyla Henya is free.

But not from her pockmarks. On Fridays, when she is bent over her rich relative's samovars and the rest of the copper and brass she is polishing in the courtyard, the little boys coming home from their day of study in heder shout at her from behind the fence, "Watch out, pockmarked Beyla Henya! The Tartar is coming to get you!" Then they run away, frightened by their own voices.

Once, in another part of the shtetl, Beyla Henya passed a house and heard two little sisters arguing. "You Beyla Henya you," shouted one of them, "you're a pockmarked mouse!"

Covering her pockmarked face with her snow-white kerchief, Beyla Henya hurried on.

Afterwards, crouching in her corner in her rich relative's servants' quarters, she pulls out her broken, rubbed-out mirror, and sees eyes that look at both sides of the world at the same time and pockmarks, pockmarks, and more pockmarks. The guests are already in the dining room and she is being called. "I'm coming," she says, hiding the mirror as if it were a stolen object and lowering her eyes as she enters the room, ashamed to look people in the face. They all know that she never wanted the Tartar even as a bride and that her dream has always been to marry a man she can look up to. In the dining room, cracking nuts, they amuse themselves at her expense: "Well, what's new with Beyla Henya? When is she marrying her rabbi?"

The rich relative has a cook, a maid, a peasant girl, and a nursemaid, all of whom are desperately anxious to get married. With every challah they bake and sometimes even with the chicken fat they render for their mistress, they make a wish. They attend every wedding in the shtetl and when the bride happens to be a bit on the older side they really get into the event. They follow the klezmer band to the bridal canopy and stay through the entire ceremony, from beginning to end. Afterwards they stand outside the wedding hall and clap to the music until the early hours of the morning. When they finally return to the servants' quarters, exhausted, they can't fall asleep, so they talk. Invariably an argument ensues; the housemaid says that the cook's husband was a thief and died in jail, the cook shouts that she knows who the maid meets every winter night behind the fence. By the time the peasant girl and the nursemaid have their say no one knows how the quarrel began and what the argument is about. In the morning, still angry, they continue to shout at the top of their lungs. The cook forgets to watch the pots and pans and lets the contents run over onto the stove. She spits in Beyla Henya's face. When the mistress comes to settle the quarrel the cook claims that Beyla Henya gets on her nerves with her talk about marrying a fine man whom she can respect: "It's really annoying to hear such an ugly creature talk like that."

These incidents repeat themselves over and over again and they make Beyla Henya miserable. But finally she is mollified, convinced that good luck will somehow find her. She has always been too stubborn and dense to see her situation for what it is and lives in a dream world of hope woven out of desire.

IV

Beyla Henya remembers a radiant sun on a hot summer day in the shtetl. It was a market day and wagons filled with bunches of onions and chattering peasants streamed in, one after another. "Eggs are cheap," they call out. Riding on one of the wagons is an old Jew dressed in his Sabbath gaberdine and wearing a velvet hat with a scruffy, worn-out rim. It is old Dovid Layzer, teacher of the youngest boys in the one-room heder in the adjoining shtetl, who is being bounced around in the broad-shouldered peasant's cart; his brittle bones rattle as he smokes his short pipe and smiles into his yellowish gray mustache. He has come to buy a new tub and a cutting board for noodles, sent on this mission by the neighbor who has been baking bread for him ever since his wife died ten years ago. He wants to pray in the local Kontikozev synagogue; he comes from Kontikozev and has never felt at home with the melodies in the synagogue in Rachmestriv where he lives. Over the years he has become very quiet, content to smile into his short gray beard and his yellowish gray mustache.

And what a silent man he is! For years old Dovid Layzer has hardly spoken a word to anyone. Yet on this morning, as he approaches the ancient Kontikozev Synagogue and hears the familiar hallelujah melodies (a bit rushed because it's a fair day), he is elated. And when he enters the synagogue and they recognize him from the old days, he can hardly contain his excitement. Not that he answers their warm greetings in so many words—he only smiles. But the smile is accompanied by a peculiar sound that seems to pour out of his ordinarily silent, tobacco-encrusted throat: khe-khe-khe. He's played a joke on the world; everyone thought that he was dead and buried, and here he is, still alive and kicking, a veritable Cossack: khe-khe-khe.

After prayers he drinks a brandy with the local congregants in the synagogue and tells his old friends that he's been a widower for ten years. "Ten years? How come? A man in your position?" they ask and even as they are talking to him Yonah Beanpole has an inspiration. Wrinkling his brow and scratching his shoulders against the wall, he tells the old man that he has an important matter to discuss with him. Before long Yonah Beanpole's wife is in the rich relative's kitchen talking things over with Beyla Henya.

Beyla Henya, wearing her new calico dress which had been sewn for the New Year holiday, is excited and her long, pockmarked face is flushed. The fair day is shot through with shining beams and her heart is filled to overflowing. She is waiting for Yonah Beanpole's wife to come again, this time to tell her what his answer is—yes or no.

That evening in the rabbi's house, where the bridal canopy has already been set up, she surveys the room with her crossed eyes and sees him for the first time. She likes what she sees. He has stooped shoulders, which give him a dignified air, and he looks very wise as he draws on his short, bark-filled pipe and smiles into his beard. He has the expression of a good-natured child being tickled by his older brother and enjoying it.

Beyla Henya also remembers how Dovid Layzer left her to return to his shtetl on the day after the wedding and that she remained at the home of the rich relative. Everyone knew that something was wrong. She felt like a laughingstock and was ashamed to look people in the face; it was a disgrace.

The rich relative, not being overly fond of her own kind, said that such a thing could only happen among Jews. She waited a week, and another week, and then she hired a peasant and put Beyla Henya and all her belongings on his wagon. "Off you go," she said, "home to your new husband."

V

Beyla Henya remembers being on the peasant's wagon and hearing the servants laughing and whispering behind her back. She also remembers how strange the new shtetl seemed to her on that summer evening when she first saw it from a distance, nestled at the bottom of a mountain near a little stream. Women, all strangers to her, were driving their animals home. Men, on their way to the synagogue, stopped to look at her as she rode through the shtetl with the peasant, wondering where she was heading. The peasant turned into a narrow alley between two half-collapsed houses, and being an outgoing type he shouted out to all the women, "I've brought a wife for Dovid Layzer!"

She knows at once which of the dilapidated houses belongs to Dovid Layzer. He is surrounded by a group of little boys who are handing him coins for tuition, which he puts into the pocket of his greasy vest. When she enters, he dismisses the children—but he doesn't look up at her. He smiles into his yellowish gray beard and stands with his back towards her, drawing thoughtfully on his half-lit stubby pipe and mumbling to himself, "Psheh!"

Then he goes off to the synagogue, as he does every evening. When he returns he finds the house tidy and clean, the bed made, the floor swept, and the old black kettle boiling on the stove. He sits at the table and drinks tea by the light of the lamp, smiling and silent as always. He is delighted and might even have shared this feeling with her, but he doesn't know her name. She is bashful and sits by herself in the kitchen near the stove; even after he puts out the fire and goes to bed she remains in the kitchen, her hand over her heart, watching the flames die.

After that Dovid Layzer never again put the tuition money into his vest pocket but would place it on the crooked windowsill for Beyla Henya to use when she went shopping in the market, just like all the other wives. By now all the women know that she is pockmarked; but they also know that her husband is a respectable man and they often ask her advice: "What do you think? Is this fresh?"

Her answers are always very brief. Beyla Henya doesn't talk much, but she knows how to cook. Old Dovid Layzer is in seventh heaven. "She must have learned how at the rich relative's house," he thinks. They both eat from the same dish, dipping their spoons in silence and not looking at each other.

Once Beyla Henya found a bargain at the market—a pumpkin, a big yellow pumpkin, so heavy that she could hardly carry it home. She cooked it with a lot of butter and millet and all kinds of spices, just as they did at the rich relative's. When old Dovid Layzer came home from the synagogue and smelled the wonderful aroma he was amazed: "How in heaven's name does she know that I like pumpkin?"

Devouring the first plate of pumpkin quickly, he holds out his dish for more, and then more. He smacks his lips and licks his fingers, looking into the pot to see if there is any left. She brings him another portion and then another and he can't get enough. That day he speaks to her for the first time: "A delicious dish," he says, "a wonderful pumpkin."

Beyla Henya feels her pockmarked face turning red and she has to go into the kitchen for a while. Her head is reeling—she has felt what it is to be happy for the first time in her life. But that evening he goes to bed earlier than usual and he is so cold that she has to cover him with two quilts. He has a stomachache—and by the middle of the night the pain is so severe that the neighbors are called in. They place warm cloths on his stomach and hot water bottles on his feet; then they bring the surgeon who pokes his hot belly with his icy cold fingers and stares into his face as if he were looking at a billy goat. By dawn old Dovid Layzer begins to feel a little better and dozes off. But an hour later he screams out in pain again.

The neighbors light the lamp near his bed and the men hurry home from the bathhouse, still wet, to read at his bedside from their thick prayer books. Dovid Layzer's sister-in-law, Keyla Malka, is hysterical. When they carry him out of the house on the narrow slab she screams and cries uncontrollably and follows the men to the funeral. The women are barely able to drag her back into the house. They stay with her and try to calm her. Beyla Henya sits alone in the kitchen, too embarrassed to look people in the face.

VI

After that Dovid Layzer's sister-in-law, Keyla Malka, and her husband, Yoysef, come to live in the house. Beyla Henya continues to live in the kitchen, in a corner by the oven.

When the husband and wife whisper together in the adjoining alcove, Beyla Henya sometimes strains to hear what they are saying. She's afraid that they want to force her out. No one knows how much money she has; they say that she managed to save a bundle from her work as a servant in the rich relative's house.

On the morning of the new moon before the New Year holiday, she goes to the cemetery right after morning prayers, just like all the women.

She is still very quiet and as thin and bony as ever; and she continues to hide her pockmarked face under her white kerchief and to avert her crossed, shame-filled eyes so as not to look people in the face. At the cemetery she walks on the farthest, most hidden path and sits for a long time near the fence, looking about her like a lost nightingale. She plucks bits of grass and listens to the women on the other side of the fence crying and tearing at the graves of their dead husbands.

Finally all is quiet. The tearful women have left the cemetery and the gate is locked once again.

It seems to her that a very long time has passed since they recited the morning prayers in trembling voices and blew the first blasts of the year on the ram's horn. She climbs over the cemetery fence and stands alone among the gravestones. Spotting Dovid Layzer's grave she goes over to it. But she has nothing to say to him; she was only married to her husband, the teacher, for three months, after all. Whenever she thinks of him she sees him as he was that evening, picking up piece after piece of the pumpkin she had prepared, his fingers greasy, clucking as he gulps down the hot delicacy, "A delicious dish, a wonderful pumpkin."

Now he lies with the best people of the shtetl. She looks at his grave for a long time, thinking of him. And suddenly she begins to keen and wail, just like all the wives who mourn their dead husbands, "You liked pumpkin . . . so I made you pumpkin."

Everything is silent in the cemetery. The crickets jump up and down in the high, untended grass. The sighs of the wailing women still hang in the air, muted, like echoes from afar. The rows of deserted gravestones look very knowing, as if they can hear Beyla Henya weeping, "You liked pumpkin . . . so I made you pumpkin."

Impoverished

I

When the waste and dreariness of her life become too much for Zivia, the younger and more embittered of the two unmarried Pozis sisters, she stops eating and washing. Wearing only her shift and a bandanna tied around her unkempt hair, she attacks the house in a frenzy of cleaning, sweating and panting as she works. The large salon that no one ever uses now gets special attention. With the greatest care she wipes the yellowing wallpaper and scrubs the walls and the balcony until they shine. When someone speaks to her, she doesn't respond; if she is called into the dining room for dinner, she flies into a rage.

Often she won't even drink a glass of tea and stays in her unmade bed all day, sometimes two days, sobbing pitifully and crying out in desperation, "God in Heaven, we're rotting here before we're even in our shrouds! This is a living death!"

The older sister, Rochele, who never leaves her side when she's like this, takes it all to heart. She is thirty-four and short, with a delicate mustache above her upper lip. Through the open window she sees their neighbor, the cooper's wife, straining to pick up a tub full of laundry. Her dress is torn and hitched up in front and she tries to balance the tub on her high belly while she carps continuously at a grubby little girl who keeps getting underfoot. Rochele can see her thick, swollen lips move up and down but can't hear what she's saying. There are tears in Rochele's eyes and she bites her knuckles, unable to stop thinking about Zivia even for a minute. "Dear God in Heaven, what does Zivia want from my life? Zivia, Zivia, do you know what you're doing? Zivia!"

As she repeats these words she remembers all the other times. It mostly happens after the Pentecost holiday when summer is approaching and the thick walls of the old neglected house begin to sweat and smell musty. The house is sinking into the damp ground and the bricks, which have become spotted with white lime, give off the sour-sweet odor of clay being baked in the factory.

This is the time of day when the house is quiet and cool. Old Mr. Pozis, the father of the household, lies on the sofa in the dining room. He is blind. His sightless eyes are covered with a white film and he blinks nervously when he hears Zivia sobbing in her room. "What is she crying about in there?" he wonders.

Bored, he scratches his head and his gray beard and lets out a long, loud sigh through his twisted mouth as he mutters weakly, "Oh, dear God and Father, King of the Universe"

The old man is waiting for Yekusiel, the bookbinder and inept beadle of the Sadegerer Synagogue, to come join him in a glass of tea. As they pass the time of day together the beadle is sure to bring up the subject of his daughters. "They have no luck, poor things." Then he'll report the news around town and finally the conversation will turn to himself, Kalman Pozis, and his former business affairs. Again he will tell him the story of the time he bought an entire forest for a song—the Zavalina, it was called. It seems like only yesterday.

"We cut down a lot of trees in the Zavalina—for twelve years we cut down trees and made a lot of money. You know, Yekusiel, Kalman Pozis was considered a very clever man once, very clever. But when the wheel turned it was his wife Leah who became the smart one; she had rich relatives. Now his children think he's a fool."

"Eh—what will Yekusiel say to that?"

Yekusiel is a nice man and not unintelligent, but he doesn't talk much. He has a handsome flaxen beard, a close-cut mustache and large, impressive flaxen eyebrows. Entering the room with an amiable expression on his face, he smiles at old Pozis from a distance. "There's nothing much new, Reb Kalman. What can be new? Things are bad; it's hard and bitter to be so poor on this long summer day."

All at once the old man is flustered; is Yekusiel referring to himself or to the old, impoverished Pozis? For a while he just lies there feeling worthless and blinking his opaque, sightless eyes in embarrassment.

"Sit down, Yekusiel."

"Thank you, Reb Kalman."

A pause.

"Things were different once, eh, Yekusiel?"

"Yes, they were different."

"Those days are gone now, Yekusiel."

"Gone, Reb Kalman."

The old man is lost in thought.

"How old are you, Yekusiel?"

No answer.

The old man would like to know what the world looks like and what Yekusiel looks like, too—he hasn't seen anything for twelve years.

"Yekusiel," he asks cautiously, like a person who is walking on tiptoe, "do you have gray hair yet, Yekusiel?"

But Yekusiel is gone. He could feel that something was wrong and that there was no chance of getting a glass of tea today, so he left early. Old Pozis is alone in the large dining room again, listening to Zivia's melancholy weeping. He is bored, bored to death with waiting.

In the late afternoon heat the shadows grow longer on the paved streets of the shtetl. The mailman, sweltering in the scorching sun, might be stopping at the house at this very moment to leave precisely one hundred and fifty rubles and the usual note: "On orders from your son I am sending herewith, etc."

The envelope is from Shmiel, his only son, who owns several distilleries somewhere near Yekaterinaslav and who sends a monthly check for living expenses. The mailman never comes except to bring Shmiel's letter once a month. The summer days seem endless—and Zivia is crying. The old man scratches his gray head and beard and with every long, drawn-out sigh he mutters, "Oh, God in Heaven—oh, dear God."

II

Something happened. There is a letter from the rich son, Shmiel, inviting Zivia to come for a visit. His daughter-in-law added a few words, too: "Zivia won't regret it! And she needn't worry if she doesn't have the proper clothes."

It's as clear as day—they have a match for her. And there's no doubt that if Shmiel and Broche like the prospective groom he's sure to be somebody special, someone who's looking for character and family and not just a pretty face.

The old man lies on the sofa, feeling gratified and blinking his opaque eyes in excitement. "What then? Wasn't it clear all along that Shmiel would find her a groom?"

He's beside himself with curiosity about the prospective bridegroom and even more about the groom's father. There must be a few words about this in Shmiel's letter and he tries to coax the girls into reading it to him.

"Rochele, darling, tell me again how many distilleries Shmiel has," he pleads, knowing that the girls think the world of their brother. Over and over again, he repeats, "As a young man he was a Hasid—right after the wedding he went to see the rebbe with his father-in-law. And now they say that he wears kid gloves and shakes hands with rich noblemen. He's bound to have a thick black beard, Rochele, don't you think? A thick black beard."

The girls are convinced that it was their late mother, Leah, who had the brains in the family and that their blind father is a fool. They don't say a word to him about the family and respectability and their expressions seem to say "Just look at whom we have to answer to."

For a few days the house is filled with unrestrained excitement. The local seamstress, who used to be Rochele's friend, is always in Zivia's room, sewing and offering advice. She has three children already and her face is covered with brown spots from her fourth pregnancy. Raised in the city by a rich step-grandfather, she is self-confident and talks as if she's an expert in the art of attracting grooms. She claims to know some useful charms and herbs for the purpose.

Finally, Zivia is ready to leave. A hired driver waits in front of the house with the luggage and Rochele is there, too, her pathetic, slightly crossed eyes brimming with tears of yearning and repressed envy. She pats the cushion: "Zivia will be comfortable sitting here."

But four weeks later Zivia is back. She is exhausted and her face is sunburned, as if she'd taken the cure. Now her heart is filled with even more despair and she has a terrible headache on top of it from the long night without sleep in the coach.

Stepping off the carriage with a smile, she seems happy to be home. The house has a holiday air about it; there's a clean yellow tablecloth on the dining room table and the family is drinking tea. Zivia, frowning, complains of a migraine; the week-long wedding celebration at Shmiel's rich father-in-law's house was very noisy.

"Oh my, oh my," she moans, "it was ear-splitting. Whenever the door creaks I think that the klezmer band is still scratching away."

The old man lies on the sofa at the side of the room, his blind eyes blinking quickly.

"Well," he asks, "and how are things in their house? He's rich, eh? They run a lavish house, eh?"

No one mentions last month's letter from Shmiel. Zivia sleeps late, but when she wakes up she can still hear the roaring in her ears. Every time the door squeaks she imagines she hears the band playing or the train whistling.

The summer days are long but the house is cool. Lonely and bored, the old man yawns as he lies on the couch in the dining room, scratching his head and pulling on his beard. And with every long, drawn-out sigh he mutters, "Oh, God in Heaven—oh, dear God."

It seems as if nothing will ever happen in this house again.

III

It is just before sunset on a clear, beautiful day late in summer. The old man is lying on his couch, waiting for his daughter to help him into his Sabbath gaberdine and take him out for a walk. Not long ago his old partner, Yisroel Kitiver, died and left a lot of money to his grandson, Notte Hirsh. Now he's busy refurbishing his grandfather's house and extending a balcony into the market.

Blind old Pozis imagines himself standing there in his Sabbath gaberdine, pointing his stick at the house and saying: "Look here, Notte Hirsh—I remember that there was a deep ditch in the very place where you're planning to extend the balcony. You'd better dig down and see if the foundation will support it."

And the people from the shtetl who are watching say, "Well, what do you think? He knows what he's talking about. Kalman Pozis has a lot of experience in building houses."

The old man can hardly wait to get to Kitiver's house in the market.

"Rochele darling," he calls out every minute, "where is my Sabbath suit?" But Rochele doesn't answer.

Something happened! A telegram has arrived. The messenger handed it to the sisters through the open window and took off. It's from Shmiel, the wealthy son. In two days' time, on his way abroad for the cure, his train will stop briefly at the nearby railroad station and he wants the family to come to see him.

This is surely a portent of good things to come. Suddenly everyone talks at once; a holiday spirit has replaced the usual gloom, and hope has been restored—forever and ever. Shmiel's telegram must surely be linked to the letter he sent at the beginning of the summer when he invited Zivia to his home. He's probably bringing someone with him—he can't be traveling alone.

Rochele's pained, slightly crossed eyes well up with tears and she is so overcome with emotion that she can only smile and say, "Shmiel! It's been eight years since we've seen you!" And calling out his name, she has the feeling that he's in the adjoining room.

All the next day the sisters work—they bake ginger cookies, wash handkerchiefs, iron their white jackets. The windows are wide open. The servant-girl watches as Rochele curls her hair and the old man, lying on the couch in the dining room, hears the sisters singing in the back room where they are pressing their clothes, running back and forth between the stove and the table with the hot iron. Yekusiel, the inept beadle from the Sadegerer Synagogue, is with the old man.

"Shmiel was a good Hasid, eh, Yekusiel," he says. "Right after the wedding he went to visit the rebbe with his father-in-law. And now Shmiel is rich—very, very rich."

Then he becomes thoughtful and silently blinks his sightless eyes, trying to picture what Shmiel looks like now. "He has a beard—he's sure to have a thick black beard. And he wears kid gloves when he shakes hands with the great lords and landowners with whom he does business, my Shmiel!"

He hardly sleeps at all that night. In the morning, wearing his good coat, he goes out with one of his daughters to the rented coach that is waiting in front of the house. But he doesn't climb on right away; first he walks around the carriage, touching it here and there—he wants to know if the seats are made of genuine leather. He imagines people from the shtetl standing around on the paved street, watching. Kalman Pozis is going off to meet his son.

"Is there a leather hood?" he asks. "Ah, there is."

The sisters, wearing their best holiday clothes, pile on all the good things they've prepared. They drive around the wide postal road, as excited as if they were going to a wedding. Everything is perfect except for the old man's constant jabbering. But when they arrive at the station they realize that they set out much too early. They will have to spend a few long hours waiting for Shmiel's train. Finally it comes. It's a fast train with reserved seats only. The conductor wears a fancy uniform and has no consideration for the people waiting on the platform. He blows the whistle twice as soon as the train pulls into the station and can hardly wait to blow the third.

"Finished yet? Eh?"

As they rush around on the platform they hear a deep, rich baritone voice shouting, "Poppa! Here I am, Poppa, standing near the window!"

A broad-chested young man with a thick black beard and shining, arrogant eyes is standing at the window. It is Shmiel, the rich son. He stretches his hand out toward his father and the old man, excited and shaking like a leaf, feels around with trembling fingers, his cloudy eyes blinking nervously. The sisters take hold of his elbows and guide his arms towards his son.

"Is it Shmiel's hand?" he asks. "Eh? Shmiel's hand?"

By now the conductor has blown the whistle for the third time and the train begins to move. The old man keeps tapping the air, as if he were still clutching his son's smooth kid glove in his hands. Finally he lets his arms down slowly.

They turn to go. The train has left the station and is far away by now, swallowed up somewhere in the furthest corner of the late summer horizon. When they climb into the carriage the sisters search the cabin; they've lost a tablecloth full of ginger cookies. But why did they bring the cookies in the first place?

No one says a word in the coach. The horses are tired and move so slowly that the bells around their necks hardly make a sound. But even the faint tinkling gets on Zivia's nerves and she cries out, "God in Heaven, those bells will drive me mad!" When they get to a wider part of the road she makes the driver stop and remove them.

In the west, over a little wooded area, the sun is about to set. There is a flowing stream in the distance, clear as crystal—pure amber. A short, rosy stripe stretches across the sky and fades in the distance. The sun looks as if it will remain suspended where it is forever, like in Givon.

The old man doesn't say a word now, heeding his daughters' warning about his prattling. He blinks his opaque white eyes and smiles into his beard. "Psheh, they think I'm a fool," he says to himself.

Slowly and silently, without the sound of tinkling bells, they wend their way home. They are eager to be there already—the sooner, the better. No one utters a sound.

Now nothing will ever happen again in the old, neglected house. Next summer, when the thick walls begin to sweat, Zivia will walk around half-dressed and clean all the rooms. She'll stop eating and drinking and finally take to her bed—and then she'll sob her heart out. And old Pozis, lying on the sofa in the cool dining room, his narrow, opaque eyes blinking, will engage Yekusiel in conversation. He doesn't want him to hear Zivia crying.

"The years have passed, eh, Yekusiel?"

"They've passed, Reb Kalman."

"They're gone now, Yekusiel, eh? Not even a shadow is left."

"Not even a shadow, Reb Kalman—like a dream."

Departing

When I looked there was a hole in the wall . . .
and when I dug, there was a door

—Ezek. 8

I

We buried Melech in the late afternoon. Everyone in the shtetl was at the small cemetery on top of the hill and for a few hours Rakitne looked like a ghost town. The only sign of life was a droshky rattling between the two rows of poplar trees on the Berizshinetz Road. We could hear the wheels clattering over the wooden dam in the shtetl.

The droshky passes an apple tree in bloom and a small rippling brook in which a peasant woman is beating her laundry over a stone. The day is cloudy and gray and unusually chilly for this time of year. It is almost the Pentecost holiday.

Suddenly the shrill sound of a whistle pierces the air. The train bringing Melech's sister from a distant province has arrived and the funeral is delayed while a delegation goes down to meet her. She is a stranger to us, standing over the open grave near the young cherry tree, crying.

After the funeral everyone leaves silently, some alone,

others in pairs. Doctor Grabay wipes the perspiration from his face. He is chilled and his throat is sore. It is about to rain.

In the old semicircular marketplace at the center of town a crowd has gathered around a tall, powerfully built man with a long, graying, unkempt beard blowing in all directions in the wind. The man is Isaac Ber, cashier of the Rakitne forest. He loved the shy young man and had persuaded him to open a small pharmacy in Rakitne a year and a half ago. His death left him shattered.

In his youth Isaac Ber had been a serious student of Talmud and planned to become either a rabbi or a ritual slaughterer. But he is a heretic now and never goes to the synagogue any more. Everything connected with religion disgusts him, especially religious Jews. He wouldn't even go to his young friend's funeral because the body was prepared for burial by pious Jews.

Isaac Ber is telling the crowd that Melech was true to his nature up to the very end, smiling even when he lay on his deathbed with an ice pack on his heart. He smiled all his life—for his widowed mother who would never know the joy of leading him to the marriage canopy, for his own unfulfilled life, for his friend Chaim Moshe, who is determined to call God to a reckoning and find out what it was all about.

It begins to rain but Isaac Ber continues his tirade and the crowd remains with him, as much out of respect for the young man who died as to hear out the disheveled cashier who once dreamed of becoming a rabbi or a ritual slaughterer but who doesn't go to the synagogue anymore, or to funerals.

It rained all night, the first long summer rain of the

season. Every flash of lightning illuminates the tall chimney at the mill and the two golden church spires at opposite ends of the shtetl. Lit up they look strangely naked. But the old forms soon return, enmeshed as before in the web of ancient fears and dreams.

We hear the rain trickling down from the roofs of the sleeping houses and into the gutters, and every drop of rain that splashes on the stones or into the basins reminds us that one of us is gone, forever gone.

It is still raining the next morning. A hired droshky stands in front of Melech's apothecary, the driver yawning and shivering in the cold as he waits for Melech's sister. She finally comes out of the shop, wearing a fur traveling coat and carrying a man's umbrella that makes it awkward for her to climb up the high step. The two young women who have come to see her off, Melech's intended bride, Ethel Kadis, and her friend, Channeke Loyber, try to help her, but she disregards their extended hands. She heaves herself up with all her might and lands on her stomach, as if mounting a horse, and the umbrella falls in the process. Then she suddenly curls herself into a ball and lets out a long, anguished moan, "Oh, Melech . . . Oh, Melech!"

At this the coach lurches forward, leaving two long tracks in the shiny Rakitne mud. The driver can't stand tears.

When they reach the marketplace Isaac Ber stops the carriage. Arms crossed over his barrel chest, beard blowing wildly in the wind, he shouts out in a hoarse voice, "Where's the key to Melech's shop?"

Then the wagon continues on to the railway station and Isaac Ber leaves for his job as cashier of the Rakitne forest, worn and haggard after a night without sleep.

.   .   .

The rains continue. Ethel Kadis keeps the key to Melech's padlocked shop tied up in a perfumed handkerchief. It is painful to watch Ethel Kadis and Channeke Loyber dragging themselves home to rest, just as it was painful to see them yesterday, staggering behind Melech's funeral procession. They were very close to Melech, closer than anyone else in Rakitne.

The next day it rains again.

The streets of the shtetl are dark and dank and the rain makes the houses appear bent.

In the afternoon it finally stops raining.

Little peasant girls out with their geese stop to watch a pair of fat, well-groomed horses with freshly braided tails splash mud all over themselves as they pull a droshky down the main street. Just as it disappears into the horizon the sun begins to peep through the clouds.

Someone notices a memorial flame burning in Melech's room at the back of the padlocked shop and when he tells his wife and neighbors about it they rush right over to talk to the young women, afraid it might cause a fire.

Ethel Kadis, speaking in the flat, unmodulated voice typical of mourners, says she knows for a fact that no one lit a memorial lamp in Melech's room. But when she and Channeke stop by the next day the lamp on the window sill is lit.

"I didn't light the lamp and I have no idea who did," insists Channeke, who is nineteen and rich. Her mother, who died young, taught her to be polite and to be truthful, always. "Anyway, I didn't do it," she adds, anxious and paling visibly.

Later they discover that Chave Poyzner, who had just returned from out of town, was seen going into the shop the day after Melech's funeral. Chave is the clever and charming daughter of Azriel Poyzner, owner of a large department store. Yossl, his trusted retainer, was with her, holding a large ring of keys. Why did Chave Poyzner light a memorial lamp for Melech? The two had quarreled before he died and she was not on speaking terms with him.

Channeke Loyber had seen it all. She was staying with Ethel Kadis while her widowed mother was away, probably to talk to her wealthy father-in-law again about the small inheritance her husband left her. The old man is a miser and makes her sweat blood before he parts with her meager allowance. Channeke Loyber was looking out of the window— anything to avoid looking at the suffering in Ethel Kadis's eyes. That's how she happened to witness the event.

Ethel Kadis, with her dark complexion and the prominent black rings under her gray eyes, always looks despondent. She feels hopeless and this has made her bitter and silent. A year and a half ago she left her studies in the middle of the semester and locked herself into her room, refusing to speak to anyone. Everyone in town talked about it and they all agreed that she was too miserable and depressed to speak.

Then Melech came into her life, and he gave her hope. People looked at her differently; some even envied her. But now her hopes are dashed and she has trouble sleeping again. And once more she is the subject of gossip.

"Without luck a person is better off dead," people say to each other at tea. "Praeger the principal claims that she is always thinking of ways to make the world take notice of her. He may be right. She's enough of a realist to know how hopeless her situation is."

Ethel Kadis doesn't care what people think of her, or

what they say either. She hardly ever leaves her house. The one time she accompanied Channeke to her big, beautiful home it was to meet Isaac Ber and talk about Melech.

II

"There's Isaac Ber," they call out when they see his tall figure and untidy gray beard in the distance.

Isaac Ber has been the cashier of the Rakitne forest for four years and he still doesn't have any friends in the shtetl. Melech was his only friend. Whenever a customer tries to strike up an acquaintance Isaac Ber glares at him, a warning to desist. He hates anything that smacks of hypocrisy.

This has made problems for him. Five wood merchants are angry with him and so is his employer, Akibason, who expects to be flattered by his employees. All thirty-four of them fawn and fuss over him. Only Isaac Ber keeps his distance. He even fought with God. "Yes, yes, it's true. I fought with God when I was still a young man."

But when Ethel Kadis and Channeke Loyber come to visit him in the forest in their light summer frocks on a warm and beautiful Sunday, and he has just rolled a fresh cigarette, and the meadow is bathed in sunlight, and there's an odor of freshly cut wood in the air, then he's very gentle and answers their questions about Melech and his friend Chaim Moshe kindly and patiently. The young women want to know what the young men talked about and where they lived and what kind of clothes they wore and all the things they did in the big city near the forest where Isaac Ber first worked.

"If only God had blessed me with sons like that," he sighed. "I understood them."

It isn't easy for Isaac Ber to talk about Melech and Chaim

Moshe, and he raises his thick eyebrows and shrugs his shoulders in the effort. He looks like a wild, bushy giant, his arms folded over his chest, as he towers over the young women who are sitting on a fallen tree trunk. The young men came to the city to study—the younger one, tall and blond and very shy, had a smile that seemed to hide a secret he wouldn't share with anyone. The older one, redheaded and good-natured, was a brilliant mathematician. He was born in Rakitne and attended the local heder.

Both were entranced with the big city. They loved the noise and the hustle and bustle and were painfully self-conscious about their small, almost imperceptible hunchbacks.

"Our inheritance," they called it, "the patrimony our shtetl fathers bequeathed to us."

They liked going to parties and were always on the lookout for new and exciting adventures. If one of them heard about something interesting going on in the city he would hurry to tell the other. They were happy. Life was good!

Ethel Kadis, wearing a black dress, listens quietly without any discernible emotional response, the silence of a young woman who once stopped talking for two months and who recently buried her fiance. Channeke sits modestly and listens politely and attentively, just as she was taught to do by her late mother. Her eyes are riveted on Isaac Ber's long, black fingernails. He's very nice, she thinks, but why doesn't he clean his nails?

"Most people in Rakitne are little better than animals," Isaac Ber tells them. "They're harnessed and they pull."

It's hard to tell whose opinion Isaac Ber is expressing, his own or the young men's. But there is not the slightest doubt that they were enchanted with life in the big city. And this despite the dangers. Every day young women leave the Gymnasium and go into the streets. The droshkies come and go and the wheels go round and round, clattering over the stones. Are the fathers oblivious? Of course they want refined and learned sons-in-law, but their minds are caught up with the new possibilities—the smoke-belching factories and the trains that bring the people to the city and the well-stocked shops and the streams that carry wood. The big city is enveloped in fog and filled with frightening, slow-moving shadows that weave chaos in the world. Chaim Moshe once remarked that he wants winter to last forever.

"Let thick snow fall on the city and cover it forever. Let fog choke the wild screams coming from the frightening chaos. We don't need a world that destroys its inhabitants before their hopes are fulfilled."

The young men think that God didn't do right by them, not from the day they were created. He could have chosen a beautiful world for them instead of this most wretched of all worlds. But there's no point in complaining or in trying to change things. Nothing can be done. Their destiny is to walk the world like strangers, seeing and hearing everything and saying nothing, only repeating over and over again, "The silent protest, the eternal silent protest."

Isaac Ber confides that ever since he became convinced that the world will never change he's quite content to ignore it. He doesn't care if he's not invited to their weddings or their circumcision parties either. Let the fools have their fun. As far as he's concerned, they're not worth thinking about.

"Well, what do you know—here's another one," the young men say, looking at each other knowingly and smiling. And from then on they call him Mister Stranger Number Three.

The forest is not far from town and the young men begin to visit Isaac Ber regularly to exchange books and ideas.

"Take it from me, there's nothing to discuss. The world has been talked about enough already. So what's left? We can look for other, better worlds at night, when the sky is full of stars."

They buy an old, battered telescope and set it up on the straw roof of Isaac Ber's little cottage in the forest and God helps them by sending a comet for them to study. Every night they climb up to the roof, Melech and Chaim Moshe first, Isaac Ber after them. And every night his sick wife shouts reproaches from her bed.

"Old man, you're crazy! What can you be thinking of, climbing up on the roof? You're as foolish as a young boy. In all my life I've never seen a man as reckless as you."

They have not lived in peace for years because of their religious differences, and for this and for the long, dull days she has to endure in bed she curses her fate. Hoping to cheer her, Chaim Moshe and Melech present her with a new Yiddish translation of the Bible and with *Kav Hayosher: The Righteous Path,* a book of moral sermons. Chaim Moshe explains that a Jewish woman who reads the holy books continuously can earn a place for her husband in the world to come. Melech only smiles.

"The entire summer they explored the heavens," says Isaac Ber.

"And what did it all lead to? How does the story end?" the young women ask.

"What can be the end of two young men whose heads are in the cloudy spheres? Chaim Moshe, the older one with the red beard, came out of it intact," answers Isaac Ber, closing his eyes and swaying back and forth, as if in a state of ec-stasy. "He could have done very well. But he's stubborn. He doesn't care."

"And the other one, the tall, shy, blond young man?"

"One time Melech appeared at my cottage in the forest looking strange, like a different person, pale and frightened. It was clear that something terrible had happened. I found out that he had been exiled for two whole years. Several times men from the city brought him to my place in the woods and hid him in a closet."

"He lived in Rakitne for more than a year and a half. He had a little apothecary shop. He was Ethel Kadis's fiance. And he died."

Isaac Ber retreats into silence as he recalls the hot, humid day in the spring when Melech died. He and some other people—Doctor Grabay, Bromberg the owner of the farm machinery warehouse and his pince-nezed wife, Channeke Loyber, Ethel Kadis—were standing in front of Melech's small apothecary shop. Several out-of-towners stopped to ask who died, but none of them knew Melech.

Then came the arguments with the burial society about where he was to be buried. The young people wanted him buried in the elite section of the cemetery, but the older people vetoed it, saying that he died under suspicious cir-cumstances, very suspicious indeed. They finally buried him next to the cherry tree at the far end of the cemetery, near the young doctor who tried to cure himself with carbolic acid after developing consumption during his studies. There is a Cyrillic inscription on his tombstone, *A Holy Martyr, Dedi-cated to Science.*

III

The young women walk home silently, thinking about Melech and his grave near the doctor's sacred tombstone. As they climb up the ditch to bypass the dusty road the shadows of the trees become long and eerie. They leave the forest by way of a small path that is covered with grass from the ploughed fields. This takes them to a green valley and to a solitary spring, holy and peaceful. It is always Sabbath at this spring. From a small hill they can see part of Rakitne, two church towers with the cupola of the synagogue between them.

All at once they are overcome by fatigue from their long day in the sun and from the air of lethargy all around them. The rooftops and chimneys glow in the setting sun and a single church bell tolls the day's end, pronouncing the eulogy in a thin, weak tone.

"It was a lovely day, clear and warm."

Ethel Kadis has the look of a woman who knows deep down that life is mocking her, but since she can't alter her fate she remains silent and pretends indifference. Channeke Loyber, on the other hand, is effervescent. She heard that Isaac Ber was in Azriel Poyzner's department store recently to buy nails and was telling everyone that Melech's friend Chaim Moshe is coming to town.

"Is it true," she asks Ethel Kadis, "is it really true that Chaim Moshe is coming?"

"Yes, it's true," says Ethel Kadis and sinks into silence again.

Not long afterwards Fishl Richtman shared a carriage with Chaim Moshe from the railroad station and the whole shtetl knew about it almost before the bells on the droshky stopped ringing. Chaim Moshe went straight to Isaac Ber's house in the forest.

Fishl Richtman had studied at the Gymnasium in his youth, but now he lives in the old part of the shtetl at the bottom of the hill and deals in sacks, like his father-in-law. Holding his baby, he tells his wife that Chaim Moshe is as pleasant and good-natured as ever. Right after they exchanged greetings he said to him, "Don't you agree, Fishl, that a man's problems grow along with his beard?"

"Yes, you're right. But how would you know, Chaim Moshe? I never said anything to you."

They were both silent for a few minutes, each thinking his own thoughts, and then Chaim Moshe asked, "Tell me, Fishl, what did Melech die of so suddenly?"

"What do you think he died of? What does everyone die of?"

"So," replied Chaim Moshe, giving Fishl a suspicious look, "you think that everyone dies the way he did, eh? Don't you believe that people die of other causes?"

Someone who walked past Isaac Ber's cottage in the forest overheard him shouting:

"No one in town really knew Melech, not even the two or three young women who were always with him."

"All right," replied Chaim Moshe, laughing, "let's say, for argument's sake, that you're right. Then tell me what he wanted, Isaac Ber."

.   .   .

The light in Ethel Kadis's room is on even later than usual that night. All the other houses on the street are dark, asleep like the people inside. Outside it is silent. No one is in the street except Praeger, the principal of the Talmud Torah.

Chave Poyzner was in love with him for years, ever since she was sixteen, but recently they broke up. Now she's about to become engaged to young Dessler from Berizshinetz, owner of the big new brewery. Praeger is on his way home from the Brombergs', still sweating from all the tea he drank. He was the life of the party, spewing out his anger at Chave Poyzner and her father.

"He's really brilliant when he gets on that subject," they whisper to each other and beg him to continue.

Now, walking at a leisurely pace, he is pleased with himself for having been so clever. When he sees the light in Ethel Kadis's window he stops to squeeze his pince-nez with the three middle fingers of his right hand, convinced that this motion inspires deep and brilliant thoughts.

If only someone would pass by now he would point to Ethel Kadis's window and prove that she *wants* people to know how much she suffers. Otherwise she wouldn't leave the light on in her room. Praeger looks up at Ethel Kadis's window again and smiles as he squeezes his pince-nez even tighter; she has brought the lamp even closer to the window now.

IV

Almost as soon as Chaim Moshe arrived in the shtetl he met some childhood friends. The driver had parked the droshky in the marketplace and while he was helping another passenger with his bags a group of bearded men came out of their shops to greet him. They had been to heder with him and recognized him even through his beard. Chaim Moshe, looking a little hunchbacked in his jacket, climbs down with a smile on his pale face and a twinkle in his eyes. He is happy to see his old schoolmates, with whom he spent so much time together in heder as a child. They are all married now with families and have become heavy and slow moving. He even recalls their childish nicknames.

"My, my," he says, jokingly measuring one man's beard, "it's more than two hand-spans long."

Someone else, now a butcher, still has the same red spots on his forehead and under his left eye that he had as a child. Everybody stands around smiling foolishly until the man with the red spots starts a conversation. "I've heard that you're writing books on mathematics. Imagine that!"

"Now just a minute," says Chaim Moshe, as he climbs back into the carriage, "there's no reason to make fun of books on mathematics. A lot of intelligence and knowledge go into them."

The carriage is beginning to move so he has to turn around and shout to make himself heard.

"Take dominoes, for instance . . ."

And suddenly he catches sight of a beautiful young woman standing on a carved balcony. She is tall and slender and a little bent over her high heels. Their eyes meet for a brief moment before Chaim Moshe turns away—a quick, instinctive movement that is also oddly casual. She has very large, slightly protruding eyes and an intelligent expression on her face, made somewhat arrogant by her half-smile.

"That's Chave Poyzner, the most beautiful woman in Rakitne," answers the driver, trying to decide whether or not to whip the horses into motion. "She was in love with Praeger, the principal of the Talmud Torah, but now she's engaged to young Dessler from Berizshinetz."

"Young Dessler?"

The name echoes and reechoes in his mind until he arrives in the forest and sees Isaac Ber and his wife waiting for him in front of the cottage. They spend the evening talking about Melech. "No one in Rakitne really knew him," shouts Isaac Ber at the top of his lungs, and when he sees Chaim Moshe smiling he becomes even more agitated.

At midnight Isaac Ber shows Chaim Moshe to his room on the other side of the house and tells him all he knows about Dessler. He's from out of town, he studied engineering, he built the big new brewery in Berizshinetz, and he owns a large share of the four-viorst peat bog in Ritnitz. He also mentions that Chave Poyzner lit a memorial lamp in Melech's room, even though she wasn't on good terms with him before he died.

"Tell me more about how Melech died. Why did he die so suddenly?"

Isaac Ber raises his hands in a gesture of defeat. He won't talk about it, or can't.

• • •

The next morning Chaim Moshe is up before sunrise, awakened by the spicy fragrance of the forest, and the strange bed. He dresses quickly and steps out into the thick, overgrown brush in front of the house just as the sky is beginning to turn gray. New place, new luck, he thinks, as he feels the heaviness drain out of his body and his movements become lighter. On the other side of the house they are still asleep.

The area near the window is neat and clean, except for a single sheet of paper covered with numbers in Isaac Ber's hand that had dropped on the block of wood serving as a step. A horse in a small open stall behind the house shifts from one leg to the other as it chomps on oats from a bag tied around its neck. Every once in a while it raises its head and looks around.

Chaim Moshe climbs over the forest gate, which is bolted by a rusty, broken lock, and walks to the shtetl. It's good to be up early. He hasn't been back to Rakitne for sixteen years and this will give him a chance to look around. He wants to see how much the fire had damaged the old house that his father sold before he died.

The shtetl has changed a lot. It is much larger and more developed and there are some splendid new houses, without names on the doors, built after the railroad station came to Rakitne. Chaim Moshe stops briefly in the old marketplace to look up at the carved balcony where he saw the beautiful, slender young woman yesterday. Then he continues on to the lower shtetl.

But the corner where his house stood is empty. Nothing is there except an overgrown lot. He stares at it for a while, thinking about his childhood, and a favorite game suddenly comes back to him. Making sure that no one is watching, he marches back and forth across the lot looking for the sentry boxes in which he used to play as a boy. Finally, his shoes soaked by the early morning dew, he gives up his search. Nothing is there but a half-buried, rotting post with a hole at the center. It reminds him of a decaying wisdom tooth. So this is it, he thinks, this is all that remains of my father's house. And he turns back in the direction of the forest.

The sun has risen and the peasant women on the other side of the shtetl are already out on the main street with their animals. Chaim Moshe smiles when an elderly Jew approaches him at the rose-colored patio next to the agricultural machinery warehouse.

"Why are you looking at me like that, my friend?" he says. "I'm no stranger in Rakitne. Tell me, to whom does the warehouse belong?"

"To whom does everything around here belong? To young Bromberg, of course. Everything on this corner belongs to young Bromberg."

Chaim Moshe heard about Bromberg yesterday from the droshky driver, who was only too pleased to share his views with a Gymnasium graduate. Not only is young Bromberg very rich, he was told, but he also serves on the board of the Talmud Torah. He's quite a man, young Bromberg!

The old man wants to know where Chaim Moshe comes from and if he has family in Rakitne. When he hears who his father was he is delighted, "Israel's son? I knew Israel well." Then, staring at Chaim Moshe, he says something totally unexpected. "Eh, you're no longer a young man, isn't that right? You must be at least thirty-two, maybe even thirty-three by my reckoning."

Chaim Moshe smiles and continues on his way. How absurd, he thinks. What difference does it make to the old man how old I am? He has it all wrong anyway. I'm not as old as he thinks. Don't the Jews of Rakitne have anything better to think about than how old people are?

He quickens his pace. Meeting the old man has spoiled his plan of getting back to the forest by sunrise to have tea with Isaac Ber before he leaves for his office at the other side of the forest. By the time he reaches the gate Isaac Ber is gone. His wife isn't there either. She took the horse and wagon and went to the next village to buy fruit to make

preserves for Akibason. Last night Isaac Ber argued with her
about it, "I say that you have no business making preserves
for him. It's not our duty to provide him with preserves just
because he owns the forest."

But she turned a deaf ear.

V

Chaim Moshe watches the pines swing gently to and fro under the bright blue sky. Every now and then a branch snaps
up, as if startled, and then immediately snaps back and sways
gently with the others once again. The red-curtained windows are open and Chaim Moshe listens to the rustling of the
leaves as he lies on his bed in his shirt-sleeves. As long as no
one is home he may as well try to get some sleep. He feels
edgy, probably because he got up too early.

But as soon as he shuts his eyes he sees the image of the
old man with the sallow, wrinkled face and the greenish watery eyes, like wet stones washed up on the seashore.

"You're probably not so young any more, eh? I mean,
you're still as free as a bird, aren't you? Why did you come
back to Rakitne?"

The old man's questions make him uneasy. Wearily Chaim
Moshe turns over and opens his eyes. Then he begins to
shout, as if he's addressing another Chaim Moshe, a worthless
young man deep inside himself who is the real target of the
old man's questions, even the unstated ones. Well, at least I
don't have to torment myself any more.

And without changing his position he tries to make sense
of the experience. The old man's watery green eyes stand for
eternity looking on with indifference as young men grow old
without fulfilling their desires. The old Jew is the anguish of

the passing generations. If he saw me manning the barricades with my party comrades, what would he say? Probably nothing at all. He would simply open his tobacco tin and take an amiable pinch of snuff in my honor. The old man means nothing to me. The best thing is to forget his squinty eyes and his questions. If I had my youth to live over again, would I listen to him and open a grocery store here in Rakitne? Nonsense! Of course I wouldn't.

The business of the grocery store has unsettled him. He remains on his bed in the clean, freshly whitewashed room with the low ceiling and the new clay floor. A strong odor of grass wafts towards him through the open window, harbinger of the coming Pentecost and of festive days ahead in the shtetl. The short red curtains flutter in the breeze and the green branches swing to and fro. The forest is abuzz with a dynamism of its own.

He is sure about one thing. He would like to stroll in the forest with Chave Poyzner and talk to her as if he were still a passionate young student. She will sigh and talk about the melancholy melody of the forest, and he will say that the melancholy melody is the counterpart of the eternal silence of the wretched world. Why did she look at me that way in the marketplace when I was with my old heder friends?

If those young shopkeepers were really important to me, those fathers with their beards, I would invite them into this room right now and tell them my simple story. But only one thing about me really interests them. They want to know whether I've "changed." Perhaps my story will divert them for a while.

I taught mathematics for six years in the big city and have many letters from grateful students thanking me for helping them pass their entrance examinations to the Institute of Technology. For the most part, however, I taught Gymnasium students, mainly young women. I always behaved very correctly with them, never permitted them to digress. They thought I was a talented, overgrown boy. What do I think of them? Why is my room always so neat? Why do I have all those brushes and tonics on my washstand? Really, it's not worth talking about. Everyone in the big city was certain that I never loved anyone, but they were wrong. I loved my father very much. You must have known him. He lived in Rakitne all his life, a very religious, very intelligent Jew. Wherever he went he carried the Midrash on Psalms with him, and his own explication of Ibn Ezra was nothing short of brilliant. Making money was never very important to him. He loved learning. After his second wife died he sold his house and sailed to Palestine for two months. It was the dream of his life, he wrote in one of his letters. He only regretted that he couldn't afford to take a trip to Alexandria, Egypt, too.

As long as I live I will never forget that day, the day the letter arrived. It was three o'clock on a hot summer afternoon and the world seemed emptied of everything, even of the gloom that always hovers over it like a fine mist. The sky and the earth and a tree in the distance looked as if they were melting in the sun when the sound of a train whistle suddenly punctured the world's emptiness. It was a locomotive climbing the hill on the other side of the big city, far from the railroad station. I'd never heard that whistle before.

And do you want to know what happened next, shopkeepers?

A young, blond Gymnasium coed was having a private lesson in my room. My hands were folded on my lap and I bent towards her. What is *a* plus *b,* squared, I asked, in

Russian, of course, but in the chant used for reading the Talmud. Do you want to hear more, shopkeepers?

I had a friend who was three years younger than I. His name was Melech and I was helping him prepare for his examinations. We both knew something about the misty spheres, from studying on our own and with Isaac Ber. In the evenings we used to take long walks. Often we searched the skies for new stars from Isaac Ber's roof. Melech loved the stars, though he never spoke about it. Oh yes, he was quite an expert at keeping silent, about himself and about the stars he loved. One day I said to him, "Just go on like this, Melech, keep everything to yourself and in the end you'll have kept your whole life inside."

And this is how it was between us, alone and together. Melech didn't agree with me when I said that each one has to wander alone, like a shadow, through this unworthy world, and each one has to die alone, too. I think it's best to die far from home and be buried at night so that no one except a passing stranger who happens to see the casket being jostled on the roughly paved street knows that another victim has succumbed. This is an allegory of the eternal silent protest.

Melech, tall bashful Melech, was drawn to every beautiful house with a pretty girl of marriageable age inside. Not that he wanted to be there and not that he went, but there was a pull. I know that he trusted me, but I always had the feeling that deep down no one really touched him, no one was really important to him. Not even his widowed mother. Once he went to visit her in his old shtetl where she has the tax concession on pots, and when he returned he had the same shy smile on his face as when he left. Nothing changed him, nothing moved him. His widowed mother just shook her head, despairing of his ever bringing any joy into her life.

When the train made a stop on his return trip he got off and crossed over to the other side of the station where the horses and wagons were parked. He saw a beautiful town nestled among the trees on the hilltop and was hypnotized by the colored rays shooting off some broken glass on one of the rooftops.

"Are you, by any chance, Lipsky's son-in-law, the engineer?" asked a driver, waking him out of his revery. "I was sent to fetch you."

Melech smiled when he told the story.

That summer he spent hours pacing back and forth in his room every evening, so lost in thought that he would forget to light his lamp. Who knows, perhaps he was thinking about Lipsky's son-in-law, the engineer? Once when I waited for Melech under his open window, listening for hours to his slow, steady tread, up and down, up and down the room, I called out, "Melech, why do you feel that you have to carry the whole world on your shoulders?"

He lit the lamp and smiled shyly as he looked down. "Don't laugh," he answered, "there's more than a little in what you say."

After that, Melech joined the movement and became an active member of the party. Then he was banished for two years, and he was so ashamed that he never wrote. When he was finally permitted to return, he settled in Rakitne. Isaac Ber helped him set up a small apothecary shop, where he sold herbs and medicine. From time to time people visiting the big city would bring me greetings from Melech and one day I received the astounding news that he was engaged to a student from the shtetl.

I was still as busy as a bee, gathering honey in the big city. As soon as I had enough I planned to share it with Isaac

Ber and Melech. Now we're all here, but Melech is in his grave three weeks already. Why did they bury him at the edge of the cemetery, right next to the young doctor who poisoned himself? Isaac Ber has aged. He seems broken and drained. It was really unpleasant to hear him arguing with his wife about the preserves yesterday. And I? Perhaps the old man is right? What *am* I doing in Rakitne? Do I have ulterior motives of my own in coming here?

The next morning Chaim Moshe leaves the forest again and by eleven o'clock he is strolling on the main street of Rakitne, walking-stick in hand. He looks distracted, as if he isn't quite sure whether he is in the forest or in town and asks every passerby where Oyzer Loyber lives.

But there aren't many people out in the heat of the day. The rooftops are red-hot under the scorching sun and the entire town seems to be in a state of suspended animation.

When Chaim Moshe reaches the old semicircular marketplace there isn't a single horse and carriage in sight. No one is there except Azriel Poyzner, the wealthy businessman, standing at the entrance of his department store. He has the velvet-like skin of an over-refined priest and from time to time he coughs gently to test his lungs. Many years ago he had respiratory problems and his round, glistening face still shows the effects of the rich eggnogs and butter cakes he ate then. He isn't alone. His beautiful daughter, Chave, is standing behind him, leaning on his shoulder and smiling, as if to say, I'm taking care of Papa, protecting him from the wagging tongues of people who don't like him.

All at once Chaim Moshe turns left, in the direction of the Berizshinetzer Road. It has been a confusing day. Early in the morning, while he and Isaac Ber were drinking their tea, a young coach driver came to the forest to buy wood—cheap, of course. He told them about the first time he saw Melech. It was in the railroad station, right after the night train pulled out. The lights on the platform had already been turned off and there were no customers around so he took his whip and went over to talk to the other drivers. That's when he noticed the blond young man standing in the corner near the boxes of mail and the wooden crates filled with grapes. Melech seemed embarrassed. Perhaps he was planning to continue on the next train.

"Can I take you to Rakitne, Pani?"

Melech didn't answer.

"Why so quiet, eh, Pani?"

VI

Oyzer Loyber's stately house on the Berizshinetzer Road is surrounded by a lovely grove of young poplar trees that adjoins the rolling meadows at the edge of town. It shines resplendently in the early morning sunlight. Strangers who pass the house are invariably impressed.

"What a beautiful house," they say, "very unusual for such a small town!"

They admire the heavy cornices under the white roof and the long glazed windows. When the house was new the local artisans used to gather there every Sabbath in their frock coats and marvel at the workmanship.

"What do you think of Oyzer Loyber's windows? They're really something, eh!"

But by now everyone in town is used to them.

The high-ceilinged, glassed-in porch is stifling hot, but the house itself is as fresh and cool as after Passover when the windows are first opened after the long winter and the birds can be heard singing in the nearby trees again. A seamstress, who has been sewing in the house for weeks, is bent over her sewing machine in one of the side rooms and Channeke Loyber and her little brother Motik are in the large dining room. Channeke is trying to get the curly-haired seven-year-old to eat his breakfast.

"Faster, Motik! Come on—one, two, and three."

At the count of three Motik is supposed to open his mouth and swallow a spoonful of food. He resembles his deceased mother, whose portrait hangs on the wall, looking down at them with pale blue, olive-shaped eyes and reminding them that she had been someone special, whom the whole town mourned. Under her maternal gaze Motik is expected to drink his cocoa without spilling a drop on the new blue tablecloth. But the little boy insists on drinking from the saucer. He will drink from the cup only if Channeke allows him sit on his knees and slurp, and without a napkin, too. Channeke moves the cup out of the child's reach, exposing a strip of white flesh at the back of her waist. She is very tense this morning and didn't have the patience to close all the hooks.

Suddenly she turns pale. There is someone at the front door and she is frozen with fear.

"Shh, Motik," she whispers, and only when she hears the maid saying that Oyzer Loyber is not at home does she dare to breathe again.

There's a story here: Not long ago Oyzer Loyber threw Channeke's tutor, Brill, out of the house. The talented, handsome, twenty-three-year-old student had been Channeke's tutor for several years and everyone in the shtetl was sure that they would get married. But that was before he attacked Leah, the black-haired seamstress who is sewing in the house right now. Channeke hasn't seen him since, but she heard that he had returned to the shtetl and is living in a rented room on the other side of town. He studies day and night, hoping to stamp out the ugly gossip by swallowing one thick volume after another.

Ever since he returned Channeke gets palpitations whenever she hears a knock at the door. But it's quiet again in the vestibule and Channeke returns to Motik and his cocoa. "Never again. You can be sure that I'll never take you to Ethel Kadis's house with me again," she says, lifting the cup to Motik's lips.

A few minutes later there are more footsteps in the vestibule and Motik and his cocoa are forgotten once again. This time it's Chaim Moshe, who has come to pick up the key to Melech's shop that Ethel Kadis was to have left for him yesterday before setting off for her grandfather's house. A telegram had come saying that he was declining rapidly. Channeke, forgetting about the exposed skin at the back of her waist, has invited Chaim Moshe to sit with her at the dining room table. She has never seen him so close before, and is disappointed. He looks better from a distance, she thinks, fluttering her long, dark lashes.

At first the conversation is somewhat stilted.

"Ethel Kadis forgot to leave the key yesterday," says Channeke Loyber. "It often happens that a person has a specific purpose for coming and forgets about it in the course of the visit."

As their eyes meet she feels that he is hiding something from her, yet at the same time he seems to understand what she's trying to say, as if he's heard it all before. Embarrassed, she lowers her eyes.

Just then little curly-headed Motik comes running into the room, crying. He has hurt his finger.

"I have just the thing to help you," says Channeke. "Place both your hands over your heart and look up at the ceiling. Then stamp your foot three times, hard."

Motik does what she says and is instantly cured. Smiling, he runs back to the sewing room, his cheerful voice echoing through the large, well-appointed, under-used house. Meanwhile Chaim Moshe is engrossed in one of the many portraits of the mistress of the house, who looks down at him with her blue, almond-shaped eyes. Channeke is shocked.

"This is the very portrait that Melech was drawn to the first time he came to the house," she says, and the conversation immediately becomes livelier. "No one in town judged Melech correctly. No one guessed that he would open an apothecary shop in that small refurbished red house at the edge of town."

He must have had all the drugs and chemicals brought in at night because one morning the pharmacy was completely equipped with a sign over the entrance, a red curtain on the window, and a bell at the door. This was just when Ethel Kadis came back, without finishing the semester. She and Channeke Loyber were out walking and when they saw the pharmacy they decided to buy some small items, soap and toothbrushes.

Melech, with his tall good looks and short blond hair, immediately appealed to them. He wore the most unusual cufflinks, which rattled like bones whenever he moved his hands. Every time the young women asked him the price of an item he checked his book of receipts, which he kept open on the counter. "I can take such and such for it."

"Can't you make it a little less?"

"Yes, I can charge a bit less," he said, studying his receipts again.

His voice was warm and deep, but a bit restrained, as if he had stifled it for years and had only now decided that the time had come to speak up.

"I felt at once that he was an interesting person, a very interesting person," remarked Channeke.

Ethel Kadis was silent. She had stopped speaking and only rarely answered questions people put to her. Mainly she stayed by herself in her room in her mother's house.

Channeke is not at all like her friend Ethel Kadis. She loves to talk. As she chatters, her beautiful bluish-gray eyes become sad and dreamy. But that doesn't stop the flow of words that pour out without any apparent effort on her part. Chaim Moshe is enchanted. He sits at the edge of his seat, unable to take his eyes off her. He can feel the soft, velvety carpet under the worn soles of his summer shoes. The pale and emaciated face he saw reflected in the large, polished mirror that he passed in the glassed-in vestibule is too thin and too emaciated for this rich house. Still, he can't stop looking at Channeke.

"What about Melech?" he suddenly bursts out. "Can you tell me what he died of, Channeke?"

At this she pales and becomes silent. Then, standing up, she whispers, "Oh, yes, the key for Melech's shop. You'll probably want to stop at Ethel Kadis's house for the key."

VII

No one paid much attention to Melech when he first came to Rakitne. Everyone was busy with his own affairs.

Channeke has an album with the inscription "Life is a sea of loving trifles and of joyous, hidden desire." On her birthday one of her acquaintances added, "Everyone casts a net into the sea and everyone finds consolation."

But a person might also withdraw the net after many years and discover that it is empty, that there is no reward. Well, so be it, the person says. I'll manage without consolation, without joy in my heart. And that person comes to Rakitne, where no one knows him, and opens a small pharmacy.

"Yes," he says to his customers who haggle with him about every small purchase, "a little less will be fine."

He is a pleasant, quiet person who accepts people for what they are. During these warm summer evenings he stands outside the door of his little pharmacy and watches the people walk by. In Azriel Poyzner's department store on the other side of town there is a constant stream of customers going through the heavy iron doors. Melech's shop is empty except for Chaike, the servant at the inn, who brings him his meals. She is all dressed up and prances around the shop in her high boots, eager to share her gossip with Melech.

"Well, how are things? Did you find someone to do your cleaning yet?" And as they go outside together she shows him her thumb, which she claims throbs every once in a while.

Leaning against the wall and smiling his shy smile, he looks as if he's warming himself at the oven while she prattles on and on.

"Praeger, the principal of the Talmud Torah, thinks a lot of himself," Chaike tells him, "but down deep he's nothing but a clown."

He likes to drink with Zanvil Potshter his landlord, and with Zalker the Singer sewing machine agent from Berizshinetz, and with Shaulke the tailor's apprentice, who has the job of dunning his customers for the money they owe Zalker. When Chave Poyzner, his wealthy and cultured paramour, refused his advances he didn't hesitate to ask all the local snobs to press his case and tell her that he wants to marry her. Chaike has as much faith in Praeger as she has in a cross. His talking and a dog's barking are both the same to her, she says.

She sees that Melech finds her stories intriguing so she continues. There is a young student who locked herself into her room in her mother's house two months ago and hasn't spoken a word since.

"Really?" he asks. "What's her name?"

"Ethel, Ethel Kadis."

"Ethel Kadis?"

"Yes, why do you ask?"

"Oh, no reason, really. I thought I recognized the name, that's all."

But he doesn't feel right knowing that people see him standing outside his pharmacy every evening with Chaike the maid. Rakitne is all eyes; Rakitne sees everything, even when it's dark outside and the streets are filled with the noises of night.

He begins to close up his shop and disappear for an hour or two every evening. In an old, run-down house with un-painted shutters on a quiet corner of a side street a young woman who was once a student spends her youth alone, in silence. Is anyone concerned? Did anyone attempt to help her when she came back? No. But every time a visitor comes to the shtetl he is taken to see the river and the synagogue and the cemetery on the hill. Then they take him to the side street.

"Do you see that house with the crumbling roof and the old, unpainted shutters? A young woman lives there, a student. She hasn't spoken for almost two months."

By now they have all grown accustomed to her condition and besides, they have something new to think about. A scandal. One Saturday night Oyzer Loyber was drinking tea on the balcony with some guests when he heard a loud scream coming from the row of young poplars at the edge of the heath. He rushed over to the spot and there was black-haired Leahke sitting under a tree, crying.

"Oh my God," she moaned, tearing at her clothes, "he ran away from me. He got away."

She was breathless and spoke with difficulty. The watch-man, who heard the commotion, came running from the other side of the house and seized the villain by the collar, tearing off the lapel before he escaped. The lapel was from Brill's new gray student jacket.

Since then Channeke often gets attacks of anxiety, especially when she suspects that her former bridegroom is somewhere in the vicinity. Whenever she visits Ethel Kadis she takes little curly-haired Motik along. He's only a little boy, but she feels safer when he's with her. There's always a tall, shadowy figure walking up and down the quiet side street, but as soon as she comes close he disappears. She's in a panic. Who can it be?

Late one night she saw the tall figure standing next to Ethel Kadis's door. Channeke almost fainted when she recognized him. It was the young owner of the new pharmacy. She gasped and the figure ran away, looking guilty and grinning foolishly.

This is the story: One evening Melech went to the old house with the unpainted shutters. Mrs. Kadis, the young widow, was not at home and Ethel was in her room, sitting in the dark. Someone knocked on the door but she didn't answer. Even when she saw the tall man's shadow on the wall of the living room she didn't say anything. Melech was silent, too, and stood at the entrance, too frightened to come in. After a while, however, he did come in and sat down on the couch, muttering a strange sound every once in a while. Ten minutes later he got up to leave and made that same sound again, a strangely piercing cry.

"Forgive me," he said, coming towards her with his eyes fixed on the floor, "I've wanted to tell you something for a long time. And I almost did, I almost said it."

And he disappeared.

Ethel put her hand to her forehead, utterly perplexed. She had no idea what it was all about. The next morning, for the first time in three months, she got dressed and left the house to go to Melech's pharmacy. She wanted him to explain.

At that point Rakitne began to take an interest in Melech. They noted when he went, when he came, and particularly how often he visited Ethel Kadis at her house. Would he marry her?

The first time Melech came to Ethel's house her mother, the young widow, was in Azriel Poyzner's department store, checking her account. She keeps the few thousand rubles that her miserly father-in-law gives her each month with him. Poyzner had no spare cash just then. It was just before the big fair in Rakitne and he had invested a lot of money in new merchandise. All he could do was to renew her old promissory notes. That's why he behaved more gallantly than usual. He sat with her at the little table, coughing every once in a while to make sure his lungs were clear, and acting the gentleman.

"I hear that your daughter is about to marry a very fine young man," he said.

The widow Kadis sighed devoutly, in keeping with her role as a respectable mother-in-law-to-be. "God willing, it will be so," she answered.

But why did Melech look so depressed? And why was the clever and beautiful Chave Poyzner seen in his shop so often, and always dressed in her best?

VIII

This is all that Chaim Moshe was able to learn, nothing more. When he returned to the forest that evening, tired and dejected, he had a talk with Isaac Ber.

"The spheres are not so hazy anymore. They're beginning to be clearer."

He couldn't sleep. Most of the night he lay on his bed in the dark, fully dressed, mumbling to himself.

"Are you saying something, Chaim Moshe?" shouted Isaac Ber through the thin wall.

"No," but a minute later, he continued, "Melech always looked as if he wanted to say something, as if he was just about to tell the world what he knew."

After his restless night Chaim Moshe went to Melech's pharmacy. It was the first time he was there and he was overwhelmed by a strong odor of carbolic acid and mold. And another odor, too, the odor of death. There was nothing much to see in the shop so he went into the small back room where Melech ate and slept. A sunbeam was playing with the dust over a small table covered with a black cloth and he thought, the ray of golden light is an emblem of the setting sun and a reminder that Melech, tall bashful Melech, is gone. A small, empty, gold-lined pillbox on the table puzzled him. Why was it there? And then he saw Channeke Loyber; she was standing behind him, staring at the table, too. He couldn't tell whether she was looking at the sun ray or at the little pillbox.

"Melech died too young," she said, sadly.

Chaim Moshe gave her a long and searching look, as if he had never seen her before.

"Yes, oh yes, he certainly died too young."

Then he began to rummage through the papers in Melech's briefcase, which was in one of the drawers, looking for his last will and testament. But instead of the will he found a small piece of whalebone and a long Russian letter in a feminine hand. "The devil is seductive and clever, but he might well be more unhappy than clever," it began.

It was clear that a young woman had enclosed a piece of whalebone in a letter to Melech. Even stranger was that Melech, shy Melech, kept the piece of whalebone in his briefcase.

"Is this Ethel Kadis's handwriting?" asked Chaim Moshe, showing Channeke the letter.

She blushed and turned away quickly so that Chaim Moshe would not see her.

"No," she answered, "I know Ethel's handwriting and this is definitely not hers."

Later, walking home with Chaim Moshe, she is somber.

"Do you know Chave Poyzner?" she asks.

"Chave Poyzner?" Chaim Moshe was surprised by the question and by the expression on her face. "I've met her once or twice." "What is she like? I'd really like to know what you think of her."

"What is she like? It's hard to say," Channeke answers, looking down at her feet. "Actually, I'd like to know your impression of her, especially when you get to know her better. Here in Rakitne Chave is considered a paragon, everyone likes her. Melech found her charming. Every time she walked past his shop he broke out in a broad grin. Everything about her was interesting to him. When Ethel told Melech that as a girl Chave would deliberately turn the inkwell over on her copybook so that the teacher would give her a bad grade, he only smiled.

Often, in the evenings, he would join Chave on the steps of her father's department store, where she liked to sit with her friends after closing time. Melech never sat alone with Chave. There was always a group of young people with her, laughing and joking.

"Jewish men never visit girls alone," she used to say. "They go everywhere in twos and threes."

When Chave went away, which she did frequently for a week or two at a time, the steps of the department store were always empty. Once when she was in the Crimea for a long vacation, Melech went to the post office every day to check the mail. Channeke saw him there once, so absorbed in a letter he was reading that he didn't even notice that he had forgotten his hat. When she pointed this out to him he blushed and smiled bashfully. He had left it in the post office, he explained.

At that point Chaim Moshe interrupted her, "Do you think the letter was from Chave Poyzner?"

"Wait, I didn't say that," said Channeke, blushing again.

Chaim Moshe took advantage of her confusion to ask her

another question, "Tell me, did Melech take poison before he died? Does anyone know?"

The conversation ended abruptly. Channeke turned pale and was too flustered to speak, and Chaim Moshe felt guilty for having caused her pain.

IX

Walking back through the woods, Chaim Moshe thought about Melech. He and I are two aspects of the same person, he said to himself. If I, unbending and unforgiving, want to get more out of life, I will have to develop the gentle, smiling Melech-like nature within me, to be more like Melech, whom everyone loved and who blessed the lives of everyone he came in contact with. Though to be honest, it wasn't until he died that people began to take Melech seriously, gentle, shy, smiling Melech.

And then one idea after another came to him. He felt as if lightning had struck and the excitement was dizzying. Every idea seemed more brilliant than the last, every thought more profound. As he walked through the forest he carried on an imaginary conversation with Melech.

"What is a person when all is said and done, Melech?"

"Nothing, Chaim Moshe, an experiment, nothing more."

"But what about human suffering?"

"It's all part of the same experiment, Chaim Moshe.

"And who is eternal?"

"I, Melech, am eternal because I have died."

"Do you feel more certain of that since you died, Melech?"

At this he quickened his pace. As soon as he arrived at Isaac Ber's house he searched for a pen and ink and went into his room to write down his thoughts.

Chaim Moshe wrote quickly, but the more he wrote the less sure of himself he felt. And when he read over what he had written, his initial exhilaration vanished completely. The ideas were simply not exciting. There hadn't been any point in coming to Rakitne, after all, he thought, pacing the floor despondently. And who was Melech anyway? Nothing but a nice young man, a small-town Romeo who set the hearts of the shtetl girls aflame, someone for whom Chave Poyzner lit a lamp two days after he died. But oh! Would she ever light a lamp for me?

He was agitated and slept fitfully that night. Disjointed images kept appearing to him. The intelligent, arrogant expression on Chave Poyzner's face; her large, beautiful eyes; her slender, slightly stooped figure; the letter she sent to Melech; the piece of whalebone in Melech's pocket. Why does she smile whenever she sees me go by? Why does she always look at me with that impudent expression, as if to say, It's because of me that you are here, Chaim Moshe. There was no other reason in the world for you to come. Why not be truthful?

And suddenly the town square appears in his dreams, empty except for Channeke Loyber. She is walking away from him, hurt and pale, her heart filled with sorrow. And he feels even sadder and guiltier than before.

"Beh! A plague on you. May you have eighty black years!" cries Chaim Moshe, tossing from side to side.

And the minute he pronounces these words he remembers that his father used the very same expression. So I'm nothing but a copy of my father, he thinks, totally unoriginal, a ridiculous caricature, like everyone who resembles his father.

He finally dozed off at sunrise, convinced that all his thoughts about life were nonsense and that he was nothing but an empty vessel who had wasted his life. Why, for example, did he come to Rakitne? He could have carried out his plan more easily in the big city. It wouldn't make the slightest difference to anyone if another person were buried at the edge of the Rakitne cemetery next to Melech.

Then he fell asleep again, and Melech came to him, holding the piece of whalebone and smiling, as if to say, This is all I have of the woman I love, Chaim Moshe.

And suddenly Melech was gone and Chave Poyzner was there. Not one, but several Chave Poyzners—all identical, all beautiful, and all singing with sweet, warm voices. He slept for only three hours but woke up feeling surprisingly light and refreshed, as if he'd shed a heavy burden during the night. His heart throbbed with excitement when he thought of what he'd written yesterday.

"And who is eternal?"

"I, Melech, who have died, am eternal."

Washing in front of the mirror in his room he saw his face, sunken and drawn, and a strange glow in his eyes. Now he was ready. On this quiet summer day with the blue sky overhead there was no longer only one Chave Poyzner. There were many, each carrying a little doll she pressed to her heart by day and lay gently to sleep at night.

"Loo, loo, loo," they sang with their sweet and tender voices, rocking their little dolls to sleep. Soon all the dolls were slumbering. One had a shy smile on his pale face, Melech's bashful smile.

At about three in the afternoon Chaim Moshe splashed cold water on his flushed face and went to visit Isaac Ber's sick wife. Then he put on his new suit and left for town. He was calm and composed.

From the small, overgrown path he could see all of

Rakitne in the distance. The two church spires and the dome of the synagogue, towering over the shtetl roofs, glowed in the misty afternoon sun. He was spellbound by the scene. It brought back visions of his childhood and the shades of those early years entangled themselves in his soul again. He had been religious then and his heart pounded as he thought, The oldest liar, my boyhood prayer book, is lying unread in the attic of the synagogue among the other old and dusty tomes.

Once in town he felt more animated and cheerful. Every time someone asked him what he was doing in Rakitne he smiled and said, "Nothing, just walking around," happy to give them an answer that pleased them.

But he couldn't get the picture of the green poplars next to Oyzer Loyber's house out of his mind, nor that of Channeke either. He wanted to talk to her, ask her to forgive him. But he didn't. He remained where he was, looking around and exchanging small talk with the Jews in the shtetl. No one was sitting on the steps of the department store, so he knew that Chave Poyzner was still away. All at once he felt an urge to go down to the old part of the shtetl and walk through the squalid, unpaved streets of his childhood.

"What's happening in the lower shtetl?" Chaim Moshe asks some men.

"Nothing," they answer. "What can be happening? The same mud, the same poverty."

It is almost sunset, the time of day when the narrow alleys of the lower shtetl are humming with life—noisy children everywhere and clattering wagons raising clouds of dust. He recalls being sick in bed as a child and watching the same little faces smiling at him through the golden dust, falling, falling. And then he hears another sound that reminds him of his heder days, the tedious tread, tread, tread of a sewing machine in one of the houses and the angry voice of a woman berating her grownup daughter, the breadwinner of the family, for having bought a new sewing machine on credit.

"I told you over and over again that I have no use for Zalker the agent and I won't have you buying a sewing machine from him."

And as he walks from cottage to cottage he notices a barefoot woman peek out of a doorway and then quickly pull her head in again.

"Oh, my God, I can't believe it!" she shouts. "Chaim Moshe is walking down the street!"

Immediately another head appears and then another and another. Everyone remembers Chaim Moshe, the nice little boy, who lived in one of the back alleys. Some of his relatives still live here and they invite him into their poor, sparsely furnished homes, smiling. He smiles, too, and tells everyone the same thing, "There's not much to tell, really. Life goes on, the same as before."

They all want him to stay longer, and they all have the same complaint. Things are bad since the peat factory closed in Rakitne.

Suddenly Chaim Moshe points to an old house across the street and shouts, "There it is!"

The long, curved roof looks like a frightened cat arching her back in the setting sun. There is no porch. On the high step in front of a door tied back with a rope, a tall young man with a long, thin face, wearing an old, torn housecoat, is holding an infant in his arms while a pale little boy of about three looks out from between his legs. All the suffering of the Jewish people since their exodus from Egypt is reflected in that child's sad black eyes.

The man is Fishl Richtman. In his youth he had been a

student but now he makes his living selling sacks at the railroad station twice a week, like his father-in-law. He and Chaim Moshe were in heder together and he shared a carriage with him from the railroad station.

"Chaim Moshe," he calls out from the open door in a high pitched feminine voice, "it's about time you came in."

"I'm coming," answers Chaim Moshe. "I'll be there in a minute."

But as he is crossing the street he sees an elderly relative walk in his direction. She is wearing her new brown silk kerchief in his honor and looks as if she is about to break out in a little dance. Everyone watches as she approaches him in her mincing, feminine steps.

"Well, well, well," she says. "I didn't know that Chaim Moshe was such a big shot."

Everyone is delighted to see little Pessl Zalivanski and happy that she is well enough to carry on a conversation. Her husband, blessed be his memory, had been an important man in his lifetime, an arbitrator for the rich people in the upper part of Rakitne.

She invites Chaim Moshe into her small, neat house with its shiny polished floor. Her late husband's desk stands in the position of honor in the corner of the room. Once it was the instrument of her livelihood, thinks Chaim Moshe, and now it is only a useless piece of furniture. He is very upset.

"No one knows me any more," the widow sighs as she tells him her problems. "Times are bad for everyone, so who should help me?"

"It's true that these are hard times," replies Chaim Moshe, his eyes riveted on the writing table, "and no one thinks about others."

And Pessl simply stands there, looking down at the floor.

X

People said that Chaim Moshe was very generous, that he gave her a full hundred rubles. Pessl only said that he took a genuine interest in her welfare and described him sitting at the writing desk while they reminisced together. He asked about her beautiful young daughter, who had married a wealthy man. Was she divorced?

"And what about the future, Pessl? How will you manage?" he asked.

"Don't worry. I'm no longer young and I have what I need." But what about you, Chaim Moshe? You ought to get married."

"Me? Married?"

And they had a good laugh together.

The news of Chaim Moshe's generosity reached Azriel Poyzner while he was checking his accounts in the department store.

"That's extraordinary. A hundred rubles!" he says, so impressed that he actually stops copying figures. But before long he returns to his accounts, thoughtfully moving a piece of cotton wool from one ear to the other and repeating every few minutes.

"Very fine, very fine indeed."

He often uses the expression "very fine." It suits his image of himself as a respected and wealthy merchant to whom widows and servant girls entrust their tiny fortunes. He has a wonderful way with people, including all the young people who come to visit his clever daughter.

With him in the store at this moment is Madam Bromberg's relative, a rich student from out of town who met Chave a few years ago and comes to Rakitne often to see her.

He's a polite and quiet young man who always carries a gold-monogrammed walking stick with him, a sign to the world that people like him and give him presents. He likes to sculpt. The first time he met Melech he was fascinated by his face and made a charming little bust of him that caught his expression and his gentle, shy smile perfectly. Chave Poyzner had just left on one of her trips, so he gave it to Channeke Loyber on her birthday. He had to do something with it because he was leaving for the big city in a few days. Now he has come back and is waiting for Chave in her father's store.

"Well, how are things?" asks Azriel Poyzner in his polite, self-confident way. "Are you married yet?"

"No, not yet," answers the student with an embarrassed smile on his face.

"You don't say," says Azriel Poyzner, clearing his lungs. "That's fine, very fine indeed."

And even though the heat is oppressive and he seems edgy, his tone is gentle and considerate, so as not to embarrass the young man. His eyes dart back and forth nervously in the direction of the marketplace and for the second time today he steps outside to look for the carriage that comes from the railroad station. The second train of the day should be in by now. Chave, beautiful, clever Chave went to Berizshinetz to see Dessler again, determined to decide once and for all whether he is for her or not. Two weeks have passed already. Does that mean that it's a difficult decision for her to make? Every time a train is due Azriel Poyzner waits impatiently outside his store, his hand shading his eyes as he watches for the carriage. From the distance he hears the soft tinkling of the little droshky bells and sees a horse and wagon in the distance. But the driver turns into a side street. A woman passes by, wearing a veil. But no, it's not her.

Madam Bromberg's relative from out of town, the rich student, is still inside, smoking. He hasn't had a chance to tell Azriel Poyzner why he came because every time he begins to say something Mrs. Poyzner interrupts them. She's a nice-looking woman, still young and well dressed, who covers her hair with a kerchief. Whenever her husband steps outside the store to look for the carriage from the station she joins him.

"Well, do you see anything?"

Azriel Poyzner's brow is wrinkled as he stares thoughtfully into the distance and he doesn't answer.

"You," he suddenly says to the elderly shop assistant who has been standing quietly and respectfully in back of the counter, "tell me your name again."

"Yoysef," says the old man.

"Oh, yes, Yossl. Listen, stand over there by the desk, Yossl."

And buttoning up his black gabardine, he walks down the stairs slowly, reluctantly, like someone who is obliged to call on a relative in mourning in the middle of the work week. He strokes his beard and keeps his myopic eyes half-closed, trying to avoid seeing people he knows in the marketplace as he walks to the lower shtetl.

In the half-paved marketplace in the old part of the shtetl people are getting ready for the annual fair, which takes place two weeks after the Pentecost holiday. Hammers are banging, booths are being set up, peasants are unloading their wares under the open canopies and the weather is as stifling as life in the shtetl. At the end of the alley the hapless Talmud Torah teacher is droning out biblical passages in Hebrew, followed by the translation in Yiddish. The little boys repeat, "And if, in the house, will return, the scourge . . ."

A schoolboy, fascinated by the frenzied activity, forgets

where he is and where he should be and stands for hours looking at the new stalls. Women from distant villages work with quick, nimble fingers under the shade of the canopies. They eat their meals straight from the pots they brought from home and smile at the young men who are either lovers or hired help, it's hard to tell which.

Azriel Poyzner has crossed the old marketplace and is making his way through the back alleys. The young women are surprised to see him. He's never been here before and they think it's almost beneath his dignity, especially in the middle of the week. He stops to ask one of the women something and she points to Zanvil Potashter's house, a sort of inn, located in the middle of the street.

"There's where he lives," she says. "You go in through the back door."

Praeger, the principal of the Talmud Torah, lives there. He was once in love with Chave Poyzner and still talks about marrying her—just to spite them all, he told Chaike, the maid at the inn.

.   .   .

Outside of the basement hostel Zanvil Potashter's wife is pounding cinnamon for the cakes for the Pentecost holiday. She sits on the ground near the kitchen door, as far away as she can get from the wet horse manure that is always left to dry nearby. She is short, thin, and childless. In one of the small rooms at the side Praeger the principal is resting on his hard bench-bed, wearing a blue satin housecoat and soft woolen slippers. He has just come home from a hard day at the Talmud Torah. Not only did he teach three very large classes but he succeeded in proving to the other teachers that it is possible to keep the pupils' attention even during these hot summer days before the vacation. In addition he had a final rehearsal with the children before their annual benefit performance for the Talmud Torah. He is quite pleased with himself. The Rakitne Talmud Torah, of which he is principal, is the envy of the entire area.

Everyone remembers when Praeger, young, arrogant, brilliant and agnostic, arrived in Rakitne five years ago. He drank too much, they said, though no one ever saw him drunk. Perhaps they said it because he fought with all the important people in town and told them what he thought of them.

"As far as I'm concerned you're the lowest of the low, no better than one of the poor tailors I drink with at Zanvil Potashter's inn."

But some people in Rakitne found him fascinating. When Chave, Azriel Poyzner's daughter, was sixteen she fell in love with him. Time and time again she promised her parents that she would stop seeing him. But every Friday night she went to the Brombergs' to find out if he'd been invited.

"Doesn't he have an unusual forehead, Madam Bromberg?

That was five years ago. Now Chave is a beautiful woman and she torments him, tears him apart. It doesn't bother her in the least that Chaike the maid and everyone else in the shtetl knows that he wants to marry her. She's been away for almost two weeks and Praeger finds the lovely summer days empty without her. Looking up at the ceiling, he talks to himself.

"What does Chave Poyzner want from me? She'll destroy me in the end."

His ruminations are interrupted by a quiet knock on the door. A tall, aristocratic, fatherly figure stands at the entrance, looking a bit awkward, as if he'd made a mistake and come to wish him a happy holiday on an ordinary weekday.

The unexpected visit unnerves Praeger. He forgets that he left his pince-nez on the little table and squeezes his nose with his three middle fingers.

"Please sit down," he says to Azriel Poyzner and walks over to the table to get his pince-nez.

They sit in silence for a while, trying to avoid each other's eyes, until finally Azriel Poyzner leans forward and says, "I've owed you a visit for a long time."

More silence.

Praeger is trying to get over the shock of seeing this distinguished visitor, the father of the woman he loves, in his room. He can't understand what brought him here. They haven't exchanged a word since last Chanuka, when he was a guest at Azriel Poyzner's house. It was a snowy evening and he saw a beautiful sled and two horses parked near the front door, the driver asleep. That must be Dessler's fancy Polish harness, he thought. And as he waited in the small, brightly lit corridor he noticed Poyzner's wife stroking a new fur coat that was hanging there. Wasn't that Dessler's new coat?

"Tell me," Praeger asked her, slowly wiping his pince-nez, "isn't your husband's coat made of genuine marten?"

"Yes," she answered, continuing to stroke the fur without even bothering to turn to him, "but his is old and worn."

"You and your husband were once fresh and young, too. Real people. But now you're worn out, old and worn out." And he stormed out of the house.

He never crossed Poyzner's threshold again and made sure that everyone heard the story, too. He was sure that Azriel Poyzner would come to see him one day, but now that his exalted guest is here in his room in Zanvil Potashter's hostel he feels let down. Poyzner is on tenterhooks, as if he can't wait to leave.

"I always thought a lot of you, Praeger," says Azriel Poyzner. "You have a brilliant mind and are a very good friend of my daughter's, I believe. That is why I am here."

"Well?" asks Praeger, his eyes still on the floor.

"Patience, just be patient," the older man answers, smiling. "You shouldn't be so impatient at your age."

This is his way of letting Praeger know that he is not only totally unsuitable for his daughter but too old for her, too.

"There's too much talk around town about you and my daughter," Poyzner begins. "You must know as well as I do that people have been gossiping about you two for years. You probably also know that Dessler, the young engineer from Berizshinetz, has been seeing my daughter lately. And, since you're a good friend of hers and a decent person too . . ."

"Well, what is it you want?" asks Praeger, who has reached the limit of his patience. "What can I do for you?"

Azriel Poyzner answers calmly, still smiling, "I beg you in my name, and in my wife's name, and in my daughter's name, too, to leave Rakitne soon, within the next five or six months, so that people will stop talking."

"Oh, really! In the name of your wife and of your daughter," mimics Praeger, outraged.

He looks as if he is in a state of shock as he presses his pince-nez to his nose and paces back and forth, trying to think of something to say. Finally, when Azriel Poyzner is halfway out of the gate, Praeger runs after him in his housecoat and screams, "Listen, you are really an exceptionally fine person. You and your wife and your daughter are all exceptionally fine people."

. . .

A few days later Praeger has a drinking party in his room. By now he is so indifferent to what people in Rakitne think of him that he doesn't even bother to draw the curtain or close the window. All he wants is to drown his sorrow.

"You're sitting in an exalted place," he says to the impoverished tailors who are in arrears to Zalker the agent. "Azriel Poyzner sat on that very chair a few days ago."

And everyone at the table roars with laughter without really understanding what the joke is about. Zalker rubs his hands together and smiles broadly, as if he has come upon a circumcision party quite by chance. After his fourth glass of schnapps his red face and even redder neck are covered with spots.

"We should become partners," he says, leaning back in his chair. "I'll be damned if you won't earn five times as much as you do from those tyrants who run the Talmud Torah."

Praeger refills everyone's glass.

"*L'chaim!* To life!" he calls out. "As far as I'm concerned all the big shots in the community can burst wide open."

Zalker the agent and Shaulke the tailor's apprentice find this very amusing and roar with laughter, and the Rakitne gigolo with the black, gypsy-like curls on his low forehead and the fluttering eyelids almost falls off his seat. Seeing Zanvil Potashter standing near the open door, Zalker raises his glass to him.

All the riffraff in Rakitne have a father in Praeger, thinks Zanvil Potashter. Not even a brother could be more devoted to them. Yet he has a good head on his shoulders and can read the most difficult texts. He strokes his red beard and puffs on his cigarette, blowing the smoke in the direction of the balcony. When he was a young man he attacked three Jews with a knife and was deported for five years. Since then he doesn't say much to anyone. He spends the long summer days leaning against the gate of his inn, a cigarette holder in his hand, thinking about the past and of the time he stabbed three men. And as he waits for his ten messengers to return with their horses from delivering telegrams throughout the district, he laughs quietly into his beard.

He likes and respects his lodger, Praeger the principal, but he never talks about his feelings, doesn't know how. Leaving them for a few minutes, he returns with two Sabbath candlesticks, brightly lit, which he places on Praeger's table. Does he want to add some light to the party or does he just want them to notice him?

"Zanvil," shouts Zalker the agent, "what's wrong? Why don't you sit down and have a drink with us?"

"Stay a while," says Praeger, his blue silk housecoat unbuttoned and a full glass of schnapps in his hand. He is about to deliver a lecture on man and his essence.

According to his theory man's essential humanity can be found only in people like Zalker the agent, and Shaulke the tailor's apprentice and Zanvil the knife. Zalker interrupts. There's an extra boot under the table and he wants to know whose it is, his own or Shaulke's? The boot turns out to be Shaulke's and Zalker laughs heartily, demanding a song from him to get it back. A woman in the street, overhearing Shaulke's song, scratches her head with a knitting needle. Some little boys, standing on the tips of their bare toes and holding on to the windowsill, look in. What is going on in that hot, smoky room, with the empty bottles and the two burning Sabbath candles on the table?

Shaulke the tailor's apprentice is beating his breast, in tears because he thinks that Zalker doesn't like him.

"He thinks I only want his money, but I love him, I swear I do. May I be worth less than this glass of schnapps if I'm not telling the truth. And you, Pani Praeger, are my soul, as I am a Jew. Go ahead, say what you want . . ."

After this drinking bout Praeger is as hoarse as if he'd been carousing all night at a wedding. It has rained all day and by three o'clock in the afternoon it is dark and cold. Everyone wears galoshes and the bottoms of the men's pants are muddy from the puddles and the fallen leaves. Many roofs are damaged. When the rain finally stops, the weather remains cold and windy with black clouds in the sky and trees swaying in the wind. It seems as if the warm summer has left us and will never return.

Now that the school year at the Talmud Torah is over, Praeger the principal spends a lot of time with Chaike, the maid at the inn, telling her again and again that he wants to marry her, and let Rakitne be damned.

Chaike is always dressed up these days and even with her large, toil-worn hands, she looks like a bride. She even refuses to clean the rooms at the inn. Her employer, a sick woman whose husband deserted her, warns her to stop making a fool of herself, but Chaike says it doesn't matter. She has as much faith in Praeger as in a cross.

"Praeger's talking and a dog's barking are both the same to me."

And she continues to dress in her finest and to spend her evenings running back and forth between the inn and the back gate to see if Praeger has come yet. He holds her hand hour after hour and assures her that after the wedding they will rent an apartment at the other end of town where Chaike can feed her chickens in the sun.

"Well what do you think of that, Chaike?"

And Chaike smiles provocatively and her eyes shoot darts of desire. "Praeger, the devil take you, Praeger."

XI

Chave Poyzner returned from her trip on the Friday before the Pentecost holiday but she didn't tell anyone whether she had decided to marry Dessler or not. She met her friends, as usual, in the evening on the steps in front of her father's store. Anshl Zudik, a tall, thirty-year-old intellectual who publishes articles in Hebrew journals was there. He had recently returned from Palestine. Madam Bromberg's young relative, the rich student from out of town, was there, too. Right now he isn't thinking about Chave Poyzner's marriage plans—at this moment it is enough for him to be here on the steps with her, holding his silver cigarette case and smoking one cigarette after another. He wrote some articles once, he says, that were published in a Russian commercial journal subsidized by his father.

"It's a pity that your articles are in Hebrew," he says to Anshl Zudik. "I'd like to read translations, if you have them."

The student thinks that all the residents of Rakitne are one big, happy family and that he is a branch of the family plucked out of the big city. He is friendly with everyone in the shtetl and they all call him Bori.

Whenever he comes to the shtetl and Chave Poyzner is not at home, he goes to Channeke Loyber's house and spends hours looking at the miniature of Melech.

"What a pity," he said once, "this statue could have been something extraordinary."

Melech's death has affected him deeply and he talks about it now with Chave Poyzner, who sits with her arms wrapped around her legs and her head on her knees.

"There are about nine thousand people in Rakitne," she says, giving Anshl Zudik a coy look, "yet not a single interesting person has ever grown up here."

That might have been said just to provoke him. She is not especially respectful of men with Jewish interests. But Zudik is too cool and sophisticated to let himself be annoyed by her. He studied in Beirut for a few years and in Palestine he met Brenner and other distinguished people. Everyone thought highly of his articles, though this isn't the time or place to discuss it. The only reason he spends time with Chave Poyzner is that she's pretty, and she knows it only too well. Not from anything specific he says—more from the look on his face and the crooked smile on his lips.

He doesn't even bother to comment on Chave Poyzner's castigation of the shtetl, except to say "Is that so?" before the group returns to discussing Melech and his friend Chaim Moshe.

"What is Chaim Moshe doing here?"

"Why did Melech like him so much and talk about him so often?"

"What was there about them that made Chaim Moshe and Melech seem so close, almost as if they were the same person. They were like brothers and at the same time not like brothers."

"What does Chaim Moshe do for a living anyway?"

It happened that Madam Bromberg's relative, the student, knew Chaim Moshe from the big city where Doctor

Grabay, the local doctor, had also studied. Chaim Moshe is a chemist, a chemical engineer to be exact.

"It's hard to say why he studied chemistry," says the student. "Doctor Grabay says that he has an exceptional mind and is a talented mathematician. But he never followed through. Anyone else with his talents would be famous, but he makes his living giving private lessons in mathematics. He even published two popular books for students to use in preparation for their examinations, but that didn't make him rich either."

The student is of the opinion that the hundred rubles Chaim Moshe gave to Pessl Zalivanski was more than he could afford and not in keeping with his financial circumstances.

They sit quietly for a while, but the conversation picks up again soon.

"What would happen if Melech were alive and here with us right now?" someone asks.

Everyone has the same answer. Chave Poyzner would ask Anshl Zudik and the student to leave so that she could be alone with him for the rest of the evening.

Day by day she grows moodier, but in the evening her eyes begin to glow and with every hour they become more beautiful. It is the look of someone who is waiting for a beloved guest to come. But now it is Pentecost eve and the street is swept and she is wearing her holiday clothes and the guest still has not come. She never mentions Dessler to her friends.

.   .   .

One afternoon Chave goes to see Doctor Grabay about a persistent ringing in her left ear. It is five o'clock and the doctor has just come home, tired from a long day at the Zemsky Hospital. The waiting room is stifling and the doctor shows no interest in examining her ear.

"It's nothing," he says, "nothing at all, like yesterday's snow."

Most things are nothing, most illnesses no more important than yesterday's snow to this beloved and respected doctor. He was once an esteemed speaker for his party in the big city, but now no one even remembers his name. He once had a beautiful and accomplished wife, but she left him and their clever little girl and the stifling waiting room. Now there is only a weary servant to take care of them. But he smiles, erasing the wrinkles around his youthful gray eyes and sending a signal to the world that Doctor Grabay is not to be pitied, Doctor Grabay is quite all right.

He doesn't want Chave Poyzner to pity him either, or to think he needs a nap during the day, and he not yet forty, so he pulls himself together and walks her home. Walking gracelessly on his short legs, his eyes clouded over with unhappiness, all he can manage in response to the many patients who greet him warmly is a perfunctory tip of his hat. When he spies Chaim Moshe in the distance he thinks, The last thing in the world I want is to be pitied by him.

And in the most casual, offhand way, with one hand in the pocket of his white summer jacket like in his student days, he introduces Chaim Moshe to Chave Poyzner. He wore his student cap and jacket for five long years after graduating from medical school, making political speeches for his party, the most powerful in town. He remembers a hot Yom Kippur in particular, "the big discussion day." The synagogues were filled with people praying and the courtyards were filled with young people talking. Inside they were chanting "We will give thanks for the great holiness of this day" and outside they stood in groups discussing politics. Doctor Grabay went from one courtyard to another, repeating his speech so often that he knew it by heart. Chaim Moshe was always there and Doctor Grabay soon recognized how clever he was.

What did the doctor want? Did he simply want to flatter Chaim Moshe in front of Chave? Was this a way of dealing with his chronic fatigue and obliterating the memory of his beautiful wife who left him despite all his sterling qualities?

Chaim Moshe is uncomfortable near Chave Poyzner but he doesn't know why. He had spent the day in his room writing about her and Melech, and it is a strange coincidence to find her here now, tall and stately, bending over slightly on her high, stilt-like heels. Her eyes are large and deep and very feminine, though not as prominent as he originally thought. Every time their eyes meet he turns away, remembering his first day in Rakitne and Melech and the lamp she lit for him after he died.

"Was Melech involved in the worker's movement?"

"What?"

Chaim Moshe wakes from his reverie and realizes that the three are standing in the marketplace and that Chave Poyzner is asking about the worker's movement in order to get his attention.

"Yes," he answers, without looking at her, "Melech was in jail for two years because of his activities with the movement."

"And what happened afterwards? Is that when he came to Rakitne?"

"Afterwards? It's a pity, he could have become a great man."

And all at once he is upset with himself for answering her

that way, dissatisfied with the relationship that he inherited from Melech and that he spends so much time thinking and dreaming about. When he sees Madam Bromberg's relative, the student, walking towards them he says goodbye and heads sullenly in the direction of Melech's shop, thinking about what must be done.

He wants to complete his unfinished business. He will live in the forest with Isaac Ber for a few months and see if he is capable of carrying out his mission. But right now some very disturbing letters are beginning to come from Melech's widowed mother. The bank is pressuring her to repay the loan she took to help Melech, and Chaim Moshe must find a buyer for the pharmacy and for the remaining inventory.

Every day he works in the pharmacy for a few hours, sorting out the merchandise. Often, when going through Melech's drawers, he becomes so involved in the material that he loses all track of time. He reads one letter and tears it up, then he reads another and tears that up, too. That's how he finds out that Chave Poyzner used to write to Melech every time she was on one of her trips. There's no doubt about it—in his own way Melech was a king. She always distorted her signature so that no one would recognize it, as if she were afraid that one day her connection to him would be damaging. Does this mean that Melech's tender behavior towards the rather plain-looking Ethel Kadis was not genuine? Had he simply felt an obligation, nothing more? How should one view this situation? Now he understands why Channeke Loyber was so upset when he showed her the letter and the whalebone.

"Do you think that this letter is from Chave Poyzner?" Chaim Moshe asked her.

"Now wait a minute," she answered, growing pale, "I didn't say that."

. . .

And of course Channeke Loyber would be hurt by the insinuation that she talked too much and revealed a secret that had been entrusted to her. Chaim Moshe's heart went out to her and he longed to have another talk with her, to apologize. He also wanted more details about Melech and Ethel Kadis. But she was out when he stopped by at the house on Berizshinetzer Road. She had taken little Motik to the four-storied, red brick mill located outside of town. It was being converted to a power station that would provide electricity to all of Rakitne. Oyzer Loyber was in Kiev now, making arrangements to have the equipment sent for the purpose and only the servants were in.

Little Motik's toys were spread all over the floor in Channeke's room and the album with the phrase "Life is a sea of loving trifles" was on the little polished table.

Chaim Moshe writes something in the album, waits a while, and returns to Melech's shop. The day is hot but there's a slight breeze and the tender saplings that surround the house sway back and forth. Everything seems to be asleep under the blazing sun—the animals, the houses, even the wagons. Above, in the blue sky, the clouds chase each other across the horizon while below the shadows play the same game in the street and in the marketplace. The difference is that in heaven everything is pure and golden, below the imitation is tainted and unclean.

At the end of the street a woman who is mending socks in front of her house looks repeatedly in the direction of

Melech's apothecary, curious about all the comings and goings during the past few days. Finally, she makes up her mind to see for herself and finds Chaim Moshe standing near the tall glass-fronted cupboards weighing out chemicals and putting them into little packets. He also records something in a notebook.

"Well, what do you know," says the woman, "I wondered who it was."

Chaim Moshe is so engrossed in his work that he hardly notices the woman before she leaves. The doorbell rings again and this time it is Chave Poyzner, wobbling a little on her high heels, as usual. She is wearing a simple white worsted jacket and a scarf around her head, as if she is visiting a relative or a close friend.

"Am I disturbing you?" she asks from the threshold as she gives him one of her bright and slightly teasing smiles.

Chaim Moshe is confused and has a foolish expression on his face. By the time he finally collects his thoughts she is in the shop, ready to sit on the chair he dusted off for her with his handkerchief.

"Put away that handkerchief," she says, giving him her special smile again.

He didn't even notice that he was holding it and quickly puts it away, embarrassed. Her visit is only a game, he thinks, some sort of summer amusement. But then he sees how solemn she is and that her eyes are filled with tears.

"Everything looks familiar, as if I used to shop here regularly," she says, getting up and walking towards the inner room.

"As if you shopped here and forgot to pay," replies Chaim Moshe.

"That's it exactly," says Chave Poyzner, surprised at what he said, "as if I bought something here and forgot to pay."

She sits down again and lowers her head. It's hard for her to be here. Chaim Moshe watches her in silence, thinking about her letters to Melech in the desk drawer, tied in a bundle. He remembers the contents very clearly.

"Are you staying here in the shop?" asks Chave Poyzner, her eyes still lowered.

"Oh, no."

Chaim Moshe has nothing more to do today and locks the desk, ready to walk with her to town like a gentleman. As they enter the marketplace Chave Poyzner cuts across the path leading to the local office of sanitation, which is headed by Doctor Grabay. He is walking towards them in his usual slow and heavy gait, tired and lost in thought. When he sees Chave Poyzner with Chaim Moshe he is startled at first, as if he's been awakened from a deep sleep. But soon his large gray eyes light up and he smiles, as if to say, "I understand everything and give you my blessing."

As he walks past them he turns around and smiles again, but Chave Poyzner and Chaim Moshe don't notice. They stop near the veranda, which juts out into the marketplace, each waiting for the other to say something. A little boy passes by and smiles bashfully but they pay no attention.

"Please come in," says Chave, finally, her intelligent eyes shining and a bright half-smile on her face.

"Yes, of course," answers Chaim Moshe, dreamily, and follows her into the house.

He is thinking about his writing. Why is it that every time he sees her he wants to finish his task, and the sooner the better? He must get back to Isaac Ber's house in the forest and apply himself.

XII

Walking towards the forest, Chaim Moshe thinks. Chave Poyzner was quiet because she has nothing more to reveal. Her cards are on the table. Everyone in Rakitne knows that Praeger spends his evenings holding hands with Chaike the maid near the fence behind the entrance to the marketplace. Chave loved Melech, and even though he felt duty-bound to marry Ethel Kadis, when Chave Poyzner sent for him, he went. Chave Poyzner used to leave town deliberately in order to write beautiful letters to Melech. Then a miracle happened. The miracle was called Dessler, Dessler of the swamps and the big brewery, Dessler the rich engineer. But what does that have to do with him, Chaim Moshe?

He quickens his pace. A person who has come to Rakitne to accomplish an important mission must walk quickly, he thinks.

When he reaches the forest the sun is still shining, but when he gets to his room he can't concentrate on his work.

Damn it, he thinks, Rakitne takes up too much of my time.

The windows are open and the room is like an oven. He lets down the short red curtains and lies down on the bed in his shirt-sleeves. The drawn curtains don't help. He feels the emptiness of the long summer day, the burning sun in the forest, the desultory ordinariness of Rakitne.

What a dreary place, he thinks. How did you ever manage to live here, Melech?

.   .   .

Chaim Moshe imagines himself standing near the dam at the entrance of the shtetl, watching the pathetic shadows chase their puny gold. The town itself is old and decrepit, a dead town. Mothers are feeding their children, sweating as they stuff eggs into them. A man stands in front of his department store and tries to remember how many felts he has put away in his attic for the winter. He coughs continually to make sure his lungs are clear and moves a piece of cotton wool from one ear to the other. Isaac Ber told him once that Melech spent a lot of time talking to Azriel Poyzner in front of his department store.

"There is something to be said for being sent away for two years, there's a certain satisfaction in it," Melech once told the storekeeper, smiling shyly.

"Nonsense," he had replied, scratching his beard and yawning. He never had any use for that sort of satisfaction. His thoughts were on practical things like felts in his attic.

"Still," added Melech quietly, continuing to smile, "one has to acknowledge that there are some people who think about other things besides making money."

Azriel Poyzner didn't agree. "Nonsense," he had repeated, yawning again, "fantasies and visions."

Praeger the principal passed by just at that point and immediately caught the drift of the conversation. He never liked Azriel Poyzner and confronted him in his usual arrogant manner.

"Will you acknowledge that there is someone in this world, Oyzer Loyber for instance, who is richer than you?"

Praeger, the hothead, was sure that he had trapped him for once, and he waited for Azriel Poyzner to admit that he was right. Pressing his pince-nez, Praeger watched the older man shrug his shoulders and play with the cotton wool in his ear. But Azriel Poyzner remained cool.

"Nonsense," he said, waving his hand in the air, "no one has counted Oyzer Loyber's money."

. . .

Suddenly Melech's face appears before Chaim Moshe.

"What was I trying to do, Melech?"

"Nothing, Chaim Moshe. A storekeeper likes to count."

"But why are you smiling, Melech?"

"Chaim Moshe, I'm smiling because you are always counting, too, though you count more like a devil than a storekeeper."

"What do you mean 'like a devil'?"

It's strange how clearly Melech sees it all now, from the other world. What difference does it make to the devil if God and Job fool each other? The point is that God blessed Job. There is joy in his house. The children come to visit every week, and so does the devil. He walks around the house, a spirit from another world, passionless, without any desire of his own, counting the fortunes and misfortunes of others.

"But there's a mistake, Melech, a big mistake."

Chaim Moshe is still too tied to the house where the festivity will take place. He feels responsible, the quiet protest. He doesn't want to remain in Rakitne and returns to the big city. One summer morning he gets up just like all the people in the big city and goes into the street. He likes the street in the early morning, likes to see the sun beating on the stones and the cool shadows on the walls. All kinds of people, the fortunate and the unfortunate, hurry back and forth and he, Chaim Moshe, is among them. A horse has fallen in the street and someone comes along and shoots him. In the big city there is no time to wait for a natural death,

death must be quick and sure. It's all over in a minute and no one has bothered to ask for Chaim Moshe's approval!

. . .

An old, blind beggar is tapping the sidewalk with his stick as he walks near Melech.

"I am ninety years old," he calls out. "Give me some money."

The street is filled with people walking here and there, Chaim Moshe among them. He sees a woman stopping to buy bread and after haggling a bit she pays. Suddenly she notices that her four-year-old child is gone and her face turns pale, "Where is he?" she screams. "Where's my little boy?"

A little further on people are standing around a half-naked woman. Her body is full of scratch marks and she looks mad. She tears at her tattered hair and beats her head with her fists as she tells the people her sad story.

"For years I've waited at home for God, sure that he would come one day. And he did come. I left the house for a moment this morning, for one little moment, and that's when he came."

The old, blind beggar is still there, tapping the sidewalk with his stick. He doesn't hear or see. All he thinks about is the money that's coming to him for having reached the age of ninety.

"I'm ninety years old," he says over and over again, "Give me something."

. . .

"What do you infer from all this, Melech?"

"Nothing, Chaim Moshe, except that something should be done to make the old man see again."

"But he's ninety years old, Melech, and he's lived on charity all his life."

"And what do you plan to do?"

"I have a remedy, Melech, a sure remedy. Just wait!"

. . .

Where is Chaim Moshe now? In a strange city. He doesn't recognize the street or any of the houses. He goes to the main gate of a house, rings the bell, and waits. No one comes to the door so he opens it himself and steps into the foyer, where several coats are hanging. Good, he thinks, that means that someone's here. But he doesn't see anyone. He waits for a while and then goes into the dining room. There's no one there, either, though there are glasses on the table and the samovar on the sideboard is still hot to the touch. A book lies open on the table, which someone must be reading. He looks around. Doors are open but there is no sign of life inside. He calls out but no one answers. He wants to leave but can't, afraid that a robber might come.

"What do you think, Melech. What should I do?"

"Take care of it, Chaim Moshe. Watch the house until the owner comes back."

"And you, Melech, wait! How did you get away?"

. . .

It's very strange, how everyone in Rakitne avoids talking about Melech's death. They all suspect that he died from something else, not heart failure, but nobody wants to talk about it. Channeke Loyber turns white every time he brings up the subject with her, and Isaac Ber lowers his eyebrows, shrugs his shoulders, and swears that he doesn't know a thing about it, not a thing.

"What can I say?" asks Isaac Ber. "I don't know. There were all kinds of chemicals in his apothecary."

People begin to follow Chaim Moshe as he walks around town, suspicious. Yesterday he saw three women watching him from a distance. They came closer but couldn't seem to decide whether to stop or not. Madam Bromberg, the one in the middle, looked at him haughtily through her pince-nez. Everyone knows that she is the leader in town. She pursed up her mouth as if to suggest that she made the cleverest remark possible and the world was lining up to kiss her for it. Chaim Moshe didn't know the second woman, who was short, dark-haired and had an oddly flat nose. The third woman, the youngest, was very tall and emaciated looking, as if she had recently recovered from typhus. Her name is Esther Fich and she's a student, just back from the big city for the summer vacation, exhausted. She wore a wrinkled white linen suit and had a yellow spot on her nose from a flower she had been smelling. Her thin face was pasty but her small eyes shone with a hungry fire, and there was a restless quality about her. She, more than the other two, wanted to stop and talk to Chaim Moshe. The women examined him closely as he walked past them and then, apologizing, Madam Bromberg called him back with a smile.

"Just this. We've taken on the duty of preparing an evening for the benefit of the Talmud Torah and we want to ask you to take part in the program, Chaim Moshe."

"Take part in the program? I'm sorry but I have nothing to offer. Besides, I'll probably be gone from Rakitne by then."

"In that case, we have nothing to talk about," Madam Bromberg said.

"I can't believe that you're leaving before the benefit. In fact, I can't believe that you're leaving Rakitne at all," interjected Esther Fich, sniffing the yellow flower she held as she looked him up and down. "Didn't you come to Rakitne with the idea of settling here permanently?" She had a shrewd expression in her smiling eyes, as if she knew his secret.

"I? What makes you think that?" asked Chaim Moshe, as he walked down the street with her while the other two women followed behind.

"At first Melech talked about leaving Rakitne, too," said Esther Fich, casually.

She walked at a good pace but she was as bent as a stalk of corn and her eyes were glued to the ground the entire time. When Chaim Moshe left her and went back to the forest, he tried to recall if he had let anything slip when he was with her. Esther Fich seemed to hint that she knew something about the cloudy subject, cloudy even to himself. It might be that Esther Fich was only talking, that she really didn't know very much. Still, he'd have to attend the Talmud Torah benefit now. Esther Fich was coming, and Dessler, and Chave Poyzner, so he would have to be there, too.

XIII

Esther Fich stayed at Channeke Loyber's house until the early hours of the morning. She had come to check on the napkins and tablecloths for the Talmud Torah benefit, but once she and Channeke started to talk she forgot to go home, forgot that she had a home to go to. Both her parents are dead and the only family she has left in Rakitne is an older brother, a wood merchant, and who knows how well she and her sister-

in-law get along? By morning Esther Fich was as worn out
and bedraggled as the white suit she wore, her only one.

"Here in Rakitne no one really lives or dies," she la-
ments. "Everyone just fades away."

Little Motik was sleeping when she arrived and Channeke was doing the household accounts at the dining room
table. But when she sees that Esther Fich makes no move to
leave she puts the receipts away. As they talk, the evening
turns to night and the shadows of the chandelier grow longer
and longer. Esther Fich pays no attention. Her mind is on
more serious matters. She's different from the other women
in the shtetl because she's been studying at the university for
five years and has almost completed her law degree. Every
summer when she returns to the shtetl she finds it duller
than the year before. Her only close friend is Doctor Grabay,
in her opinion the only one in town worth bothering with,
now that Melech is dead.

"There's a lock on his apothecary shop," she sighs, her
eyes two tiny, tired slits.

Her wrinkled white suit hangs on her narrow frame and
she looks like a scarecrow. But can she talk! Her mouth is
like a spout and the words flow out in torrents. Yesterday she
was at Melech's pharmacy with Chaim Moshe and as soon as
she saw the yellow pillbox in his room she understood that
everyone in Rakitne had been duped, the fools! Why didn't
anyone realize that Melech was dying, slowly and surely
dying. He took a small dose of a fast-working poison every
day for a week. Imagine how horrible it must be to take
poison every day for a week! Chaim Moshe was astounded
when she told him. How was it possible? But she was right,
of course. The only other person who had any suspicion of
this was Doctor Grabay. He recalled seeing a small, uncov-

ered, iodine-stained medicine bottle under Melech's pillow,
though he didn't pay much attention to it at the time.

During the entire time that Melech lay in bed with an
icebag on his heart, Doctor Grabay came to see him every
day. He always stayed for an hour and a half or two and then
checked his heart. It's nothing, nothing at all, he kept saying. He'll make it. Melech always smiled, and this a minute
after he had taken poison or a minute before he was about to.
He managed to fool everyone.

And where were Melech's good friends through all this?
asks Esther Fich, her eyes shooting sparks of anger. Ethel
Kadis should have been devoted to Melech and his needs, but
since she never bothered to fluff up his pillow she didn't
know what was under it. And Chave Poyzner fought with
him the very evening before he died. They say that she was so
eaten up with jealousy that she left town rather than watch
them grind the cinnamon for the wedding cakes. That's when
she went to meet Dessler. Well, so be it. But then why
did she light a lamp for him the day after he died? There
are many things Esther Fich doesn't understand. What is
Melech's friend, Chaim Moshe, doing here, for example?
They say that he spends a lot of time with Melech's former
friends.

Channeke Loyber gives an involuntary shudder, but she
says nothing, not a word to make Esther Fich less suspicious
of Chaim Moshe.

When the evening began Channeke Loyber was flattered
that Esther Fich confided in her—she is the youngest in the
group and no one ever takes her seriously. But Esther talked
so long into the night that all Channeke could think of was,
Please, please go home. The minute Esther made a move
towards the door she jumped up to accompany her, relieved

that she could finally go to bed. And then, tired as she was, she couldn't sleep. She kept thinking about herself and Esther Fich and the conversation they had that night.

Why is Esther Fich here? She's not young any more. By now she's the oldest unmarried woman in the shtetl. The only person with whom she has anything in common is Anshl Zudik, who has been to Palestine and who publishes articles in Hebrew. An ideal pair, one would think. But the truth is that they can't get along. Whenever they see each other they argue and sometimes the arguments get so violent that other people have to intervene.

.   .   .

A few nights later Channeke Loyber dreams that Melech's sister has come to Rakitne for a funeral. It is early in the evening. At the far end of the cemetery, next to the cherry tree where Melech is buried, a fresh grave has been dug for the journalist who lives with Doctor Grabay's wife in the Crimea. Edith Kadis is there, too, and joins her and Melech's sister when they approach the body. And when they look at the face before it is covered for the burial, they see that it is not the journalist at all. It is Chaim Moshe!

Channeke wakes up with a start and begins to braid her hair, a nervous habit. But she doesn't tell anyone about the dream. She doesn't believe in dreams, not in the least, even though they often seem to intrude into her life. She dreamed about her mother's death six months before it happened. And a month before their laundress gave birth to a baby girl she dreamed that she held a blond, blue-eyed baby girl in her arms.

Her dream about Chaim Moshe has made her very jittery and Channeke has no patience for her little brother.

"Motik, be quiet," she says to him. "Just go away and leave me alone."

Every time the doorbell rings she grows pale with fear, as if she expects someone to come and tell her that her dream about Chaim Moshe has come true. She's tired and has a headache and it's a hot and dreary day, the kind of day on which anything might happen.

But nothing does. She and Motik are dressed in their holiday clothes, ready for guests who never come. Disappointed, she waits for the sun to go down and as soon as she sees the shadows crawling along the sidewalk and up the sides of the buildings she leaves the house. Her temples still throb and one of her eyes is twitching. But when she enters Madam Bromberg's house with Motik she looks as fresh as a daisy and smells of sweet, perfumed soap.

They sit in the small back dining room, which is pleasantly cool despite the heat outside. Madam Bromberg knows how to make her visitors comfortable. No one mentions Isaac Ber or the forest, so obviously nothing has happened to Chaim Moshe. One of the guests, the new government rabbi's wife, "Rebbitzin" Lifshitz, who has a flat nose and intelligent black eyes, is doing some kind of handwork. The talk centers around the new express train that will soon be coming to town and the latest fashions in the big city—straight skirts, so narrow at the bottom that it's hard to walk. Channeke stays for tea but is bored. She eats only to please her hostess, her late mother's best friend. When she leaves she is as nervous and discontented as when she came, the sun is as hot and uncomfortable, the shadows as long. The wretched day seems endless.

Two employees from Bromberg's farm machinery warehouse are walking in the street, dressed in their Sunday best and sparring with each other. The peasants in the surrounding villages are celebrating a midsummer holiday and those who are left in Rakitne are bored. They miss their friends, the stall owners, who went home half-drunk. Church bells ring in the distance, refreshed after their day's rest. They are trying to decide whether to chime in unison or to chase each other through town. The crest of the hill above the deserted town is covered with a blue haze and the trees in the forest seem to reach to the sky.

Is Chaim Moshe in the forest now? wonders Channeke Loyber as she holds Motik's hand to keep him from running up the hill. Her heart is pounding and she blushes at the thought that flashes through her mind. She'd like to visit Chaim Moshe. But why? He's a virtual stranger to her—he's been to her house three times at the most, and not at all recently.

"Motik, don't run, please," she shouts irritably.

With whom is she irritable? Is it with little Motik, who is always underfoot? Or is it with herself for being drawn to Chaim Moshe?

.   .   .

At the other side of the marketplace Channeke Loyber sees Isaac Ber's wife sitting on a bench near the crockery shop.

"What are you doing here on such a hot day?" she asks.

The sickly, sallow-complexioned woman, dressed in her Sabbath best, constantly wipes her face with her silk kerchief. She looks as if she's about to faint. How did Isaac Ber let her to come to town on such a hot day? thinks Channeke.

The woman explains, "He doesn't believe in God any more. Somewhere, perhaps among the wood shavings, he has abandoned his faith. He didn't even get cleaned up for the anniversary of his father's death last week. But I'm not like him. I believe in God, and even though I'm sick I came to town to light a memorial candle."

She is waiting for the beadle to come and open up the synagogue so she can light the candle before she goes home. Isaac Ber doesn't know anything about it. He left early in the morning with his horse and wagon.

"Did Chaim Moshe go along?" asks Channeke, blushing.

She had never mentioned his name before and wonders what Isaac Ber's wife thinks about it. But she needn't have worried. The sick woman doesn't give it a second thought.

"Who? Oh, that devil? He doesn't eat, he doesn't drink, he doesn't sleep. All he does is rush around from one place to the other."

It had been her idea to invite him to visit after Passover. She thought it would do him good. But the devil locks himself into his room for hours at a time.

"I have no idea what he does there. When I ask him he only smiles. He has dark rings around his eyes and is nothing but skin and bones. And he's awake all night long, talking in his room. I can hear him.

"Chaim Moshe, who are you talking to in there?" I shout.

But he only laughs, "It's nothing, nothing at all. Only some ghosts dancing around in my room."

Isaac Ber's wife suddenly makes a confession to Channeke Loyber. She doesn't like having Chaim Moshe in their house. He frightens her—he says the strangest things. She can hardly wait until he leaves.

"Why are you so pale, Channeke?" she asks, seeing her color change suddenly. "And why are you rushing home? The synagogue is still closed. The beadle hasn't arrived yet. Oh, when will he come?"

"Goodbye, goodbye, have a good day," says Channeke and dashes off.

Her feelings for Chaim Moshe confuse her and make her anxious. She thinks of him as a wise, older brother, but closer, much closer. Her own older brother hasn't bothered to visit her for years, doesn't understand that he should. Now she feels as if he's come back. But why is he in the forest with Isaac Ber's wife, who would be only too happy see him leave? Why isn't he with her? If only she could talk about it with someone in Rakitne?

Just then she sees Doctor Grabay walking on a side street. He might just . . . after all, he knows Chaim Moshe from the big city. He could . . .

But Doctor Grabay walks right past her, his closely shaved face with its elegant patrician mustache covered with perspiration, and exhausted because he didn't have a rest during the day. But he moves quickly on his short legs as he makes his home visits. Just a minute ago he went to the wrong house and now a little girl with a sweet smile is leading him to the right address, "There, in that house," she says, "they're probably the ones who called for a doctor."

Preoccupied, he forgets to thank the child. But when he notices Channeke Loyber with Motik he suddenly wakes up and smiles brightly. "I have to go there, to that house," he says to Channeke, "but it's all the same to me. It makes no difference to me where I go."

XIV

Doctor Grabay is with the hygiene committee. He rushed through his work at the hospital and spent very little time with his sick patients before this meeting. But now he is calm as he accompanies the visiting inspector, a thin, stern, angry-looking non-Jew with blue tinted glasses. His acquaintances will get special preference for jobs.

The doctor himself wears an expression of numb fatigue. He deliberately keeps himself detached and lets the inspector make his own decisions.

For the past three days Doctor Grabay has felt as if he were a prisoner of the committee. But now, day four, the senior members have gone and he is a free man again, sitting at the table near the millstone in front of Azriel Poyzner's department store and watching the old shop assistant open a bottle of lemonade for him with the kind of flourish usually reserved for important customers or priests.

"Believe me, Reb Azriel Poyzner," he says, smiling, "it's all worth as much as yesterday's snow. The main thing is to keep up the illusion of victory, to give everyone an opportunity to feel heroic. Look, here comes a hero now."

It is Anshl Zudik. The doctor grins, which makes the lines around his eyes appear even deeper, and gives the tall man a friendly pat on the back, motioning him to sit down across from him.

Before Anshl Zudik left his house he checked his white collar in the mirror and decided that it would do. He is a skeptic with a skeptic's view of life and the world, even of Doctor Grabay. At this very moment, even while he and the doctor are talking, everyone in town is gossiping about his beautiful wife and the famous journalist for whom she deserted her husband. She has come to see her child and is probably in town right now. The doctor, who tries his best not to let the gossip get to him, talks about the emptiness of life and the worthlessness of everything, like the snows of yesterday.

He has a story about a "hero" who was recently brought to the hospital—a thin, pale, emaciated young student from a nearby town. His mother said that he studies all the time and goes without sleep for nights on end. But the young man didn't talk about his illness. He was interested only in the pictures on the wall and the books on the shelves. He has no faith in medicine or science. Medicine has no cure for a broken heart and so is useless; the laws of science aren't worth the paper they're written on; and the law is useless, too, because it doesn't serve justice. A person who breaks someone's bones is punished, but there is no punishment for a person who tramples on someone else's feelings.

"He's an individualist, a person apart, clearly one of today's heroes," says the doctor.

And does he know an engineer named Dessler, Dessler from Berizshinetz? No, he never heard of him.

"It's funny how one hero doesn't recognize another," says the doctor, chuckling in his aristocratic way and placing his hand on Anshl Zudik's shoulder in a gesture of friendship. "You see, I myself was once a hero, in a manner of speaking."

Doctor Grabay is happy to be drinking lemonade in the shade near Azriel Poyzner's department store and is in no hurry to leave. At this hour his small waiting room is very hot and there is no one at home except the tired servant and his six-year-old daughter whom his wife deserted along with him. The little girl is recovering from diphtheria and sits for hours at a time on the wooden bench in the clinic, her throat wrapped in flannel, playing with the doctor's old violin that the maid found in the attic. When he first came to Rakitne he used to play long passages from Mendelssohn's violin concerto so beautifully that passersby would stand under the window to listen. They said that it sounded professional.

Now all that is left on the violin is a single limp string that hardly makes a sound when it is plucked. That's the story of the doctor's violin.

Anshl Zudik feels uncomfortable with the doctor's arm around his shoulder and smiles awkwardly. What a quiet worm, he thinks—this courteous doctor who's always talking about charitable foundations is really only interested in making money. They say that he has thirty thousand stacked away in a bank in another town.

The doctor is telling him about the period after his graduation from the university when he was still in his student uniform and made speeches for his political party. He used to travel all over the country. In those days everyone knew him. He was a brilliant speaker and attracted huge crowds.

One summer evening when he spoke to a young audience in a large city, one of the women came up to him after the lecture and accompanied him down from the third story. She was slender and beautiful and a head taller than he, and they talked animatedly in the dark hallway. Then the doctor kissed her. What happened after that? Did he marry her? Is she the wife who left him two years ago and is back now to see her child? She is slim and beautiful, too, and almost a full head taller than the aristocratic, rather heavyset doctor, who is sitting with Anshl Zudik, leaning on his elbows and staring silently at the marketplace.

They see Channeke Loyber walking past the department store in a white summer dress and matching hat, carrying something wrapped in a shawl. The package is heavy and as she stops to regain her balance she notices the doctor and Anshl Zudik sitting at the table. She smiles as she walks in the direction of the street that leads to the forest.

This is the second time that Channeke has brought

Melech's statue to the forest, and again Chaim Moshe is out. Exhausted from carrying the heavy package in the heat, she rests in the shade near his door, flushed and perspiring. Isaac Ber's wife is there, too. Channeke talks to her about her husband, her illness, her house—anything at all as long as she doesn't have to explain why she's here. But the sick woman never asks.

Why doesn't she get better? Why won't she try other remedies, not only cupping?

The house with its clay floor and short red curtains and scent of spices and fresh green reeds contrasts strangely with the heat outside. Before she leaves, Channeke writes a note to Chaim Moshe. "I brought you Melech's small statue because I think it belongs to you more than to me. Madam Bromberg's relative, the student, won't object, I'm sure. I wanted you to have it as a gift for your birthday, but no one in Rakitne knows the date."

Reading the note makes her anxious again. Her handwriting is terrible. She never realized before how bad it is. Irritably, she tears up the note and leaves the statue with Isaac Ber's wife, asking her to tell Chaim Moshe to stop by at the beginning of next week.

XV

On Sunday the noisy, three-day summer fair opens in the old part of the shtetl. It is lively and cheerful. Festive red beads have been hung on the doorposts of the shops and the marketplace is filled with all kinds of linens and cheap calico. The shopkeepers begin to display their wares at the crack of dawn when sweaty people stream in to the fair on foot or in wagons from all the surrounding villages. Everyone coming from the valley below or from the ploughed green hills above is happy. The early summer is warm and the sky is blessedly blue.

By eleven o'clock that morning the narrow alleys of old Rakitne become quiet enough for the dreamy strains of a harmonica to penetrate. The village horses chomp on fresh hay, raising their heads high and whinnying with pleasure. In the wealthier, cleaner part of the upper shtetl there is silence, the silence of the rich at the end of a long and idle summer week. At an open window a curtain waits patiently for a breeze that never comes, and a hot, tired beggar knocks on one locked door after another, to no avail.

There's not a soul to be seen on the main street. The shtetl is full of sun and empty of people. Even the long heavy drapes on the windows of Oyzer Loyber's house near the grove of young poplars on the Berizshinetzer Road yearn for a breeze to come and move them. But the house itself is cool and fresh. Oyzer Loyber is not home yet and little Motik is driving everyone mad, kicking and crying because he's impatient to go to the fair. Channeke paces the floor nervously.

Early that morning, while everyone in the house was still in bed, someone rang the front doorbell. It might have been one of the troublemakers who bring their geese to the village green. On the other hand, it might have been a certain someone coming from the forest after Isaac Ber's wife told him about her visit. The bell didn't ring again.

In the afternoon, when the heat lets up a little, Channeke takes Motik to the fair. The little boy wants to run ahead but Channeke holds him back protectively.

"Where are you off to, you little rascal? You'll be run over yet."

Distracted, she drops one of her new gloves and her shiny

parasol just as the heavy, pockmarked Jewish cook passes her on her way home from the market. Her baskets are heavy and she is perspiring but she stops to pick up the parasol.

"Motik is so wild," she says, frowning, "he's like quicksilver. He'd creep under the horses' bellies if you'd let him."

Two rows of horses wait at the bottom of the hill near the entrance to the fair, harnessed to their wagons. They grind their teeth and swish their tails, dropping manure on the very path on which Madam Bromberg and the short, pugnosed rabbi's wife are now making their way toward them. The two are dressed as if they were at a wedding—especially Madam Bromberg, who wears a black satin coat and gold pince-nez. She came to buy a piece of calico as a present for her servant, but among all the lengths of calico on display she can't find anything suitable. These days she takes the new rabbi's wife with her everywhere and the younger woman clings to her every word. Whenever Madam Bromberg comes up with one of her witticisms she purses her mouth, waiting for the world to come and kiss it. She's always conscious of her role as the exemplar of society. Fourteen years ago she fell in love with her cousin and married him, the first non-arranged marriage in the area, and now everyone is doing it.

The three stand almost on top of the horse manure, holding their open parasols while they talk. Madam Bromberg tries to restrain little Motik. Why must he always be so mischievous?

Everyone pampers Motik because his mother died young. They know that his older brother, Buma, is a worthless, ignorant nobody who once ran away from home with a large sum of money. He was somehow involved in the scandal between Brill and Leah, the dark-haired seamstress, too. Buma is already twenty-three and they finally got him into a foreign technical school.

The women talk about Doctor Grabay's wife, who is in the neighboring shtetl. Whom will she visit in Rakitne, they wonder, looking at each other meaningfully. Madam Bromberg, no doubt. Channeke's cheeks are red hot. She has discovered that the new rabbi's wife is a close relation to Brill the student. Why does she keep staring at her? What does she want?

"If you were a good brother, Motik, you'd come home with me now," she says.

But Motik whines and pulls her even further into the crowd of people who are pushing and shoving their way toward the booth where soda water is being sold. Once caught up in the crowd there is no turning back. It's a stifling hot day and the fair smells of perspiration, smoked fish, and leather boot wax. Someone pokes Channeke from behind and knocks the open parasol out of her hand, but her corset is so tight that she can't even turn around to see who did it before she is pushed into another part of the market by the crowd. Now she is in a larger and airier section, close to the Christian cemetery near the open fields at the end of town. The sound of swishing tails and the odor of fresh manure fill the air. They've come to a horse fair.

Motik pulls her toward a young colt who is shaking and crying because he's been separated from his mother. There is a lot of noise and commotion as the animals are driven around and around in front of the wary buyers. A little further on, young Dessler from Berizshinetz is being shown two large and spirited black horses with strong arched necks and huge muscles—the attendant can hardly restrain them. He pays no attention to the salesmen who talk to him nonstop.

Dessler has small, dark, bright eyes, thin lips, and a short, blond, pointed beard. He carries an antique silver cane and wears a new black overcoat, elegant gloves, shiny patent leather shoes, and a hat made of a stiff brown material. The newest style calls for soft, black hats, but Dessler isn't one to let the current fashion dictate what he wears. Brokers follow him around, scraping and bending to get his attention, but he continues to ignore them. He's nobody's fool. He examines the horses and then consults with Yan, the young non-Jewish army officer he brought with him. He trusts him implicitly. Yan listens respectfully, always answering, No, no, not yet. Then he inspects the horses himself. He counts their teeth, examines their ears, lifts their front legs to check the hooves, runs his hand along their backs, and always finishes with a swift, hard pull of the tail that makes the horses shake. Yan works fast and the effort leaves him breathless, but he is clearly enjoying himself and looks very happy standing next to Dessler. The horses have passed inspection.

Dessler makes an attempt to smile but his longish face remains stony and impassive. He talks to the liverymen and pays with fresh new bills. He always uses new bills and always buys the choicest goods available. They say that he is about to marry Chave Poyzner, the most beautiful woman in Rakitne, and in the entire area.

Not far away Motik is crying. Somebody stepped on his foot and as Channeke bends down to comfort him she sees a carriage pulled by a team of horses and hears a dreadful scream. She shudders. People are shoving and she suddenly finds herself and Motik pushed to the side. In the midst of this pandemonium she sees Chaim Moshe's face very close to hers, dizzily close. Her heart begins to pound.

"Was it you who pushed me out of the way? Have you been standing here all the time, watching Dessler from Berizshinetz buying new horses?"

"No," says Chaim Moshe with a smile. "I was at your house. I wanted to see you."

XVI

On that same Sunday, Zalker the Singer sewing machine agent is driving his fancy, brass-trimmed carriage with the bright-colored tassels from Berizshinetz to Rakitne. He is a well-built, ruddy-complexioned, youthful-looking man who likes to wear narrow, patent leather boots. He left home at the crack of dawn to avoid the heat and is half asleep under the roof of the carriage, dozing off now and then. Every time he wakes up he is surprised to find himself holding the tan reins and the bamboo whip and driving on a Sunday morning on a road still wet with last night's dew. He has a bitter taste in his mouth from the brandy he drank yesterday, all through the Sabbath, and from the anger he feels towards his slovenly, bad-tempered wife in their godforsaken house in Berizshinetz. If only he could forget about her! She's not so much older than he is, a few years at the most, but she hasn't got a tooth in her mouth—every night she takes out her dentures and puts them in a glass on the night table between their beds. That's how she goes to bed, without teeth.

Feh!

Draining the last of the brandy from the bottle, he decides to drive to the Ritnitz marshes on the other side of the

Rakitne hills. Just as he reaches the silvery Ritnitz stream he sees a wagon coming from the small village at the side of the road, heading toward the Rakitne fair. A peasant girl, decked out in her Sunday best, sits on the top, back-to-back with her father, the driver. Zalker winks at her as he unbuttons his riding coat and removes his hood. He wants her to see the shiny, lacquered visor on his cap and his peasant-like face with the elegantly trimmed, prematurely gray beard. The stern expression in his green eyes that intimidates all the tailors doesn't frighten the girl in the least and she responds to his coarse, suggestive leer with derision, blowing her nose into her hand and wiping it against the side of the wagon.

Zalker is suddenly reminded of Leahke, the dark-haired seamstress, who becomes coy and sprightly whenever she sees him lately—ever since she bought a sewing machine on time from him, just before Passover. And again the feeling of loathing for his slovenly wife overcomes him. The truth is that it was for her, black-haired Leahke, that he got up so early this Sunday morning to drive, half asleep, to Rakitne. The thought that he would be seeing her soon cheers him immensely. He goads the horse on, overtaking many heavily laden wagons as he drives down the hill. When he reaches Rakitne the wooden dikes are bathed in sunlight and there are scores of wagons loaded with produce for the fair.

The sky is a glorious blue and the earth is so hot that it burns the peasant girls' bare feet.

Zalker sees Shaulke, the tailor's apprentice, standing near the shops at the entrance to the fair. He is the one who duns the Rakitne tailors for him.

"You there," he calls out, pulling the reins back sharply. But Shaulke doesn't hear him. He is absorbed in his own thoughts and his shrewd eyes stare into space as he leans against a wagon and chews on a straw. His black hair sticks out on all sides under his crumpled brown hat and his low forehead is wet with perspiration. When he finally strolls over to Zalker, halfheartedly, the agent is looking in another direction and cracking his bamboo whip. His face is hard but his voice is hoarse and weak. He hasn't spoken yet today.

"Did Michl Kravetz pay?"

"Eh?" says Shaulke, placing his foot on the lower step of the wagon and chewing apathetically on a straw. "Ah, yes, he paid."

"And Yossl Kirshner?"

"He squared his account."

"What about the American tailor?"

"He paid right after the Sabbath."

"Wait—and the nun from Butvineker?"

"Yes, she just paid."

"And how about black-haired Leahke?"

"Well, I'm waiting for her payment," says Shaulke with a big smile on his face and a suggestive wink. "She promised, I swear she did, Pani Zalker. She said she'd pay soon."

Zalker's face turns beet-red and he stares at Shaulke with a cold and angry look in his eyes.

"You can play your tricks with the dark one after she pays! Do you hear me, you fool?"

And without another word he drives off toward the other side of the fair, calling out a greeting to an acquaintance who sells Christian prayer beads from his booth. Then he takes a detour around the fair to the road which leads to Isaac Ber's house in the forest. Isaac Ber isn't in. Only his sickly wife is at home in bed and he tells her that he's found a customer for the inventory in Melech's apothecary.

"What's the name of the young man who wants to sell the chemicals? Chaim Moshe, isn't it? Well, tell him to be in touch with Zalker. I'm staying at Zanvil Potshter's place in the old city. He can find me there at any hour of the day."

Zanvil Potshter's courtyard reeks from wet horse manure and is teeming with flies. In the attic, under the broken roof, a fat year-old baby crawls around, oblivious to the heat and to the terrible stench that makes the older residents choke. The big fair contributes even more odors and adds the cheerful sound of neighing horses and the clatter of steel knives.

Things are different at the water trough near the tarred kitchen door. The pitted floor, newly swept and sprinkled with water from a kettle, smells like a freshly mopped synagogue, and the room is as quiet and cool as a cellar where it is tempting to sleep, just to sit and doze off for a while.

In one of the rooms a tall, large-boned man in a bright shirt is repairing the keys of an accordion that is spread out in front of him on the table. The man has a wide nose that is smudged with dirt, black eyes, thick lips that seem to move even before the words come out, and a sparse beard in various shades of grey. The beard is obviously precious to him. While he works he occasionally looks up at the sunbeams above the horse manure or at the open gate, so he is the first to see Zalker riding like a lord toward the house. As the lame watchman unhitches the horse, Zalker sits on the bottom rung of a ladder that leads to the attic. He is relaxed now, his eyes riveted on his narrow, lacquered boots and he doesn't think about Shaulke, or of dark-haired Leahke, either. Later in the day he'll go to see her. Now he's not in the mood.

"Watch it!" he shouts angrily at the crippled servant.

"You're not careful enough with my two new sewing machines. Pay attention to what you're doing! Take them down slowly and look where you're going!"

Zalker is interrupted by someone clearing his throat behind him, trying to get his attention. "Ahem! Ahem!" He turns around and sees a wide nose and a pair of round, widely separated eyes that appear to come from another world, silent eyes.

"Yes, yes," says the man through thick, trembling lips, "Singer and Company. They produce a fine product. Exclusive, first class!"

Zalker can't stop looking at the man in the green shirt, the guest at Zanvil Potshter's inn who travels from fair to fair repairing accordions. Who is he, this man without a home and probably without a father either?

"Feh," says Zalker, spitting skillfully through his closed teeth, still angry. He asks if Praeger the principal is in and goes directly to his room.

. . .

The Talmud Torah is already closed for the summer and the children's benefit performance will take place in ten days. After that, Praeger is free for eight whole weeks! He is happy, happy that he dislikes the people of Rakitne no less than they dislike him, happy that Chaike the servant has been going around dressed up like a bride. Her friends say that she's crazy.

"You're a fool. In a year Praeger will leave you."

"One year with Praeger is better than a whole life without him," she answers them stubbornly.

Well said, Chaike! thinks Praeger, and he feels that she is worthy to be his bride. He is very satisfied.

.   .   .

It's a warm Sabbath morning and the entire shtetl is celebrating the sacred day. The white oven in which the Sabbath cholent stew has been warming all night is teeming with black flies. Praeger walks by the shuttered windows of the houses and hears the young women speaking courteously to one another, in keeping with the spirit of the Sabbath. Even though the men are in the synagogue, they come to the table fully dressed to drink their tea.

The streets are empty and all the shops to the left are closed. Towel in hand, Praeger strolls to the river at a leisurely pace. There are no carriages to disturb the quiet on this sunny Sabbath day. He recalls his first summer in Rakitne and smiles with pleasure. But when he passes the open windows of the synagogue on the hill and hears the worshipers chanting the old, familiar Sabbath prayers a sudden wave of anger at their stubborn conservatism overcomes him. If he smoked he would light a cigarette right now, on the Sabbath, and show those pious worshipers a thing or two. He deliberately bathes at a point in the river that can be seen by everyone in the synagogue.

But he gets tired of the game after a while and comes out of the water, drying off very slowly. By the time he's dressed the congregation begins to recite "A new light will illuminate Zion."

Suddenly he notices something shimmering in the sun on the other side of the river, a green silk cape under a pink silk parasol. Can it be? he wonders, his heart pounding against his chest. No, I don't believe it, it can't be—Chave Poyzner!

A moment later his heart beats even faster. He's sure now that it is Chave Poyzner, come for a swim. Her legs are hidden by the tall grass and she looks as if she's floating on air as she disappears into a thicket and reappears in a long white tunic. She dives straight into the river. And what a swimmer she is! It comes to her naturally. Her father often comes here on Friday afternoons and swims the entire length of the river as the little boys watch from the shore. Chave Poyzner has her hair tied back and looks majestic in her flowing white tunic as she swims along gracefully, smiling as her lovely long fingers scatter the sunbeams with each stroke.

In the synagogue they're only at "God, our Father." Praeger was mistaken when he thought he heard them saying "A new light will illuminate Zion." It's earlier than he thought and he still has time to walk along the edge of the river towards the thicket. How many years has it been since he came to Rakitne? Six. There were a lot of big old trees then, but they've all been cut down and only the roots and some short, yellowing trunks are left—they look like benches. Praeger sits down on one of them and scratches the ground with a stick. He can't get the picture of beautiful, statuesque Chave Poyzner out of his mind. It's been a long time since he's seen her up close. How his heart pines for those days, only a few years ago, when they used to meet in this very thicket. Now they're like strangers. She won't even answer his letters. He wonders if she saw him from the other side of the river.

He hears footsteps behind him, Chave Poyzner's footsteps. She's on her way home and is about to pass him on the road. Why is she walking with such heavy steps? Is it possible that she wants him to turn around? No, she doesn't even nod. She has a supercilious smile on her face and looks surprised to see him, as if she didn't know that he was still living in Rakitne. And that's all, nothing more. She passes him and, without so much as a glance back, vanishes into the night. Does she know that Chaike, the maid at the inn, has been walking around dressed up like a bride for days and that she's stopped working. The owner has been told to look for a replacement, and the sooner the better.

.   .   .

After that Saturday, Praeger notices a certain coolness in Chaike and he begins to work with renewed effort on the wedding preparations. He arranges for a band from Berizshinetz to march through town playing klezmer songs while barefoot boys and girls run ahead and Zalker the agent shoots fireworks, some sort of little matches that burn a long time. Trust Zalker—he knows where to get what he wants. For the wedding itself he has hired several fiddlers, a flutist, a clarinetist, a trombonist, a drummer, and two men who play the fife. But Chaike doesn't seem to be impressed by any of it. She's gone back to wearing her torn shoes without stockings and works as hard as she used to again. She loves Praeger, of course, and will never forget him, but what can she do? She knows that if she marries him she'll live to regret it. All the respectable people in Rakitne say so.

Praeger would like to know just who these respectable people are. In his opinion, there aren't any respectable people in Rakitne. If Chaike knows any, let her name them. But Chaike is stubborn, very stubborn. She refuses to name names.

Lately she has begun to meet Yossl, the clerk from Poyzner's department store, behind the inn after work. His eyes are slightly crossed, but he is twenty-four years old and strong and he wears shiny boots with white stitching. Once, seeing him waiting behind the inn, Praeger asked what he was doing there and Yossl bent over, picked up a straw, and jumped over the neighbor's gate and into her overgrown garden without answering.

"Well, so much for the respectable people," Praeger thought, his suspicion confirmed.

One Saturday he invited Leyzer, the twelve-year-old who left the Talmud Torah to work in Poyzner's department store, to spend the day with him. Everyone knows the chubby boy in the apron with the perennial smile on his face because he spends all his spare time standing respectfully near his boss's desk, as if he's guarding him while he copies figures from one book to another. Praeger learned a lot from the boy. He told him that Chave Poyzner, always concerned about her father's health, has become completely devoted to him lately. No one else in the world seems to matter to her. She takes over the cash register every day at noon so that he can rest, generally sitting with an open book and staring into space. One day she told Yossl the clerk that he was a fool for not marrying Chaike from the inn. Yossl turned red as a beet and didn't know what to say or which way to look, so he shouted at Leyzer for standing in the street. Leyzer just stuck out his tongue, but he heard Yossl say, "Chaike is a servant."

"You can't really call Chaike a servant," Chave Poyzner pointed out. "She was raised at the inn by Ita Leah, a sickly woman who has no children of her own. Her husband deserted her years ago and married another woman in America. Ita Leah promised Chaike that if she marries a nice young man she will leave her the inn when she dies, after a hundred and twenty years."

Chave Poyzner doesn't consider Praeger a nice young man. She herself has changed a lot. Not only is she devoted to her beloved father, the wealthy shopkeeper, but she has become considerate of others, too, and is always doing good deeds for the poor Jews at Dessler's. She feels responsible for everyone and is sure that Chaike the maid will suffer if she falls into the wrong hands.

Could Chave Poyzner be doing this for less than altruistic reasons? Could she be sorry that she gave him up? Could she be just a little jealous of Chaike? If so, he is ready to live in the hope that one day Chave Poyzner will quietly enter his room at Zanvil Potshter's inn, full of apologies and ready to admit her guilt as she used to do in the past.

And squeezing his pince-nez even tighter on his nose, he paces up and down in his room, thinking. Then he sits down to write Chave Poyzner a letter. He has always known what an accomplished person she is. He has even learned recently that she can swim. But it wasn't until now that he learned that she is capable of spoiling a match.

He is sure that she will not answer this letter either, but mails it nonetheless and goes to find Chaike at the back of the inn, too impatient to wait for evening.

"Well, how are things going? Have you thought it over, forgotten the madness? No? Really? Still stubborn, still working like a horse? Why not come right out with it and tell me that you no longer love me? Once you found me appealing, but that's all over now, I see. Do you think we could patch things up between us? I can be more respectable and stop fighting with everyone in Rakitne. I have no parents. The only person I have in the world is a stepmother and I'll write to her and ask her to lead me to the wedding canopy. Then people will know that I wasn't found behind a fence. But why the tears, Chaike? Don't you like what I'm saying? I'll stop—only answer me once and for all, yes or no.

You don't want to give me an answer before Tuesday, after the fair. Well, all right then, I have to wait."

Returning home by way of the old city, he paces up and down in his room and squeezes his pince-nez with his middle finger again. What explanation can there be for Chaike's insisting on waiting until after the fair? Does it mean that she hopes to see Chave Poyzner again and get her advice? If so, Chaike will tell her everything, including the story about his stepmother.

Praeger's heart beats very fast and he feels as if he's in a stupor as he waits for an answer. These beautiful, clear, light blue summer days are filled with memories of Chave Poyzner.

One day a letter arrives. He quickly melts the wax and sees that she has written only two Russian words, "It's licentious."

Chave Poyzner thinks that all the pretty words spoken to Chaike behind the inn are meant for her. Chave Poyzner knows that she's number one, and everyone who has ever seen her room with the white bed and the bric-a-brac around it has to agree that all the other women are only poor copies, counterfeit banknotes. Well good! It means that his connection with Chave Poyzner is not yet broken. Hurray! Long live the connection, even if it's only through Chaike the maid.

· · ·

It's now two o'clock on Sunday afternoon. The clatter of steel knives being sold nearby, the spirited neighing of horses, and all kinds of other sounds from the fair drift into Zanvil Potshter's inn. The men are sitting around the table in Praeger's room, drinking brandy out of yellow wooden mugs in which Zanvil Potshter put orange peel and herbs. Zalker and Praeger find the drink exceptionally smooth. At first it's like any other brandy but when it goes down it's like fire.

"So, what do you think?"

"Let's have another one, eh?"

"Absolutely."

They are happy, chewing on cold sour pickles and letting the juice dribble down their freshly shaved chins. But after four drinks they feel as if they are being pummeled, the blows landing on their heads like sharp, swift kicks. The clanging of the knives and the neighing of the horses seem much louder than before and the shouting and noisy jubilation of the fair have completely taken over the house on this hot summer day. Everything seems very close, almost at hand's reach. Praeger has the feeling that Chave Poyzner is near him, that she is walking around downstairs, next to his room, and a new wave of joy fills his heart.

"Wait! Where is everyone?"

"Where's the ghost?"

"Who? The fellow who repairs street organs?"

"Zanvil, bring him here."

The accordion repairer really does look like a ghost. He enters the room carrying a large accordion under his arm and sits down timidly at the edge of the bench, pulling on the few precious hairs on his chin with his long, thin fingers. His eyes are filled with gratitude at having been invited to drink with them and he smiles shyly. He can hardly believe it, and of course he's ready to leave the minute they tell him to do so.

"Where are you from, Uncle?"

"From everywhere."

"And do you drink?"

"Ha, ha, that's a good one!"

"Well, pour some for him, Zalker. He'll play for us."

"Here you are, Pani!"

After two drinks he is flushed. Legs crossed, he balances the large accordion with the polished brass nails on his bony knee and bends over it, pulling it up to his face and turning his head from side to side, as if he can't decide whether to put it closer to the right ear or to the left. And all at once the room is filled with lively melodies that dance and tumble around like little acrobats.

"What are you playing? Chopin?"

"Ha, ha! I go from one fair to the other, from village to village, to play in the courtyards of noblemen."

He takes deep breaths along with his instrument. Everyone is entranced with the music and no one notices Shaulke the tailor's apprentice standing at the door. This is the second time he has come. The first time he couldn't believe what he saw. His pockets are stuffed full and he has the expression of a thief who has been caught in the act and begs to be forgiven.

"Listen, Pani Zalker!"

The playing suddenly comes to a stop.

"Get out of my sight, you bastard!"

"All right, let me just put these things on the table."

And like a magician he begins to pull various-sized bottles filled with liquor out of his pockets. What deep pockets he has! He's already taken out at least six bottles and they're still not empty. This is his way of making amends.

"Pani Praeger," he says to the sweaty principal, "I beg you, ask him what I've done to offend him?"

"Just let him say one word, let him make the smallest peep, and I'll bring the dark one here right now. As I am a Jew, I'll go and get her. Well? Shall I go?"

Just then Zanvil appears, looking upset and signaling something with his hands.

"What is it?"

All at once everyone is quiet. Zalker gestures to his friends to remove some of the bottles from the table and put them under the bench. At the door, behind Zanvil, stands a smiling young man with sparkling black eyes and a reddish beard. He looks shocked. It is Melech's friend, Chaim Moshe, who has come to speak to Zalker the agent about the buyer for the inventory in Melech's shop.

XVII

It is impossible to carry on a conversation at the noisy horse market and finally, tired of being pushed around, Chaim Moshe takes Channeke to another part of the fair. She doesn't say a word but there is something in her sad blue eyes that speaks to his heart and fills him with the same deep, unspoken panic that she feels.

"What is it, Channeke . . . why did you come to the forest twice?"

And again her only answer is a look, silent and pleading.

"Watch it!"

Another carriage drawn by a team of horses comes up from behind and he pulls Channeke even further to the side. She shivers when he takes her arm.

"Wait! Where is Motik?"

"There he is."

And right then and there they have to buy him a shiny red wooden spoon from a barefoot peasant who has his wares displayed on a sack on the ground. And soon afterwards, when Motik sees their driver, Trochiman, returning with the freshly bathed horses and the yellow droshky still wet from being washed in the nearby stream, he starts to cry again. This time Channeke sends him home with the driver and she and Chaim Moshe walk off together. They stop to watch some bleating lambs being sheared in the sun, their legs tied together. From a distance they hear pigs squealing frantically, as if they are being trampled alive.

They have reached the very end of the fair, where the open country turns into a dusty road that leads far, far away, into the wide world. A slow-moving wagon makes its way on the road, the first of the wagons to take off at midday and escape the heat and the noise of the fair. A rebel.

"We are like that driver."

Channeke shivers again, as if waking from a dream. Could it be Chaim Moshe who said those words? Or is she only imagining that she hears someone speak? Chaim Moshe becomes very quiet, absorbed in thoughts of his own.

Walking aimlessly through an untended pasture, they come upon a field of green corn waving gently in the sun. In between the two fields is a path leading to the grounds where a forest grew, until it was razed eight years ago. A new forest of tender saplings is sprouting there now, protected by a locked gate.

They rest, sitting on the new grass next to the young forest and listening to the crickets sing.

"Chaim Moshe . . ."

She can't get the words out. Chaim Moshe takes her hand and looks at her tenderly, and at once she realizes that he knows it all. She sees in his deep, intelligent eyes that he has always known what she wants to say, that she's been here with him before and told him everything. But there is something she wants to tell him now.

"I am happy. At this moment I am happy about every-thing, even about little motherless Motik. How strange it is! I have no claim on you, none whatsoever. Please don't mind my crying. It's nothing, nothing at all, just that I was sud-denly reminded of Melech."

Her eyes shine with happiness, but she is silent all the way home. When they arrive at the door she doesn't ask when they will meet again. She doesn't need to. She knows that a new life has opened up for her and she feels very, very happy. As Chaim Moshe turns to go back to the forest she feels that he is now a part of her newfound life.

At the entrance to Praeger's room at the inn in the old shtetl Chaim Moshe thinks, I'd like to go back to Channeke's house right now and talk to her openly, tell her everything the way I used to with Melech. Praeger's room is filled with half-drunk, pale-faced men and bottles of liquor.

"Go and get her this minute, you dog. Do you hear me?" someone shouts.

The lad scratches the back of his neck and disappears.

"Where is Zalker from Berizshinetz?" Chaim Moshe asks. At this, the person with the tight patent leather boots who had been banging on the table stands up.

"I'm here about the inventory in the pharmacy," says Chaim Moshe.

"Yes, yes, says Praeger. "We're dealing in schnapps now. Don't be afraid. We're just ordinary people. Will you have a drink?"

Someone fills a tumbler for him without bothering to rinse it first and raises his glass.

"*L'chaim,* to life!"

"To your health!"

"May all the fine citizens of Rakitne burst wide open!"

"Drink up!"

The walking corpse with the misshapen nose coughs lightly, pulls on the few hairs of his beard with his long fingers, and as he moves his chair away from the table he presses on all the keys of the accordion at once to let out the air.

"You're something of a revolutionary, isn't that so?" he says to Chaim Moshe.

"A revolutionary? No, not now. I might have been once." Chaim Moshe finishes his drink and looks around for Praeger.

"What is it, Pani? Are you ashamed of it?" the accordionist aks.

Zalker pulls his feet out from under the table, leans back on his chair, and stretches his legs, showing off his narrow patent leather boots.

"Ha, ha, ha," laughs Praeger, "I have a younger brother who's a revolutionary, too. He spends all his time traveling between Kerson and Nikalayev. And what a clever fellow he is! Once I met him on a street in Odessa. 'How are things?' I asked. 'How should they be?' he answered. 'Everything will work out in time.' 'No, that's not what I meant,' I said, 'for years now you've been very quiet.' 'Don't worry about it,' said Yonah. 'Well,' I said, 'see to it that the rich get another kick in the stomach. Ha, ha, ha!'"

Praeger lies down on the bench and laughs so hard that his feet fly up in the air. He doesn't even feel the flies walking on his bald pate and high forehead. But all at once he becomes serious.

"Wait!"

His eyes are watery, his tongue feels thick, but his mind is as sharp as ever. He wants to talk, to squeeze his pince-nez and talk.

"Brave fellow!" chimes in Zalker brightly, waking up from his stupor. He pulls at Praeger's sleeve and clinks glasses with him.

"He can go to hell, the bastard!" says Praeger.

Zalker would have kissed Praeger if he let him. Praeger, his shirt still unbuttoned, gets up from the bench and shouts out, "I say *l'chaim!* Let all kindhearted shopkeepers burn in hell. Let . . . but why are you leaving already, Chaim Moshe? What's the hurry? Are your ships about to sink?"

Chaim Moshe agrees that his ships are not sinking and that he can stay awhile. He wants Praeger to know that Melech would have said something else entirely. Melech would have said that you have to take the shopkeeper out of the kind heart. But no matter. More to the point right now is the heat. He would like to sit closer to the open window. What a deafening noise is coming from the fair!

"I have my own complaints about Rakitne. I'm not so happy about things here either. If we were found dead in our beds one morning, we would be buried at the furthest end of the cemetery, near the fence. That's the way they do things in Rakitne. I just can't understand why they had to bury Melech near the fence. I've asked everyone, but no one will tell me the truth. Let's say that Rakitne disappeared from the face of the earth and only the cemetery remained. Well, Melech is the most important person in the cemetery. He should be buried at the front, in the main section. Anyway, *l'chaim!* Forgive me, Praeger, for getting off the track. I didn't mean to put on glasses, as you would say. I was thinking of an acquaintance of mine, a historian, who wrote the history of a town based on information he gathered in the cemetery. You agree, don't you, that in history, the dead are alive and the living dead. But I want to ask you something about Chave Poyzner, Praeger. I'd like to know more about her. I have my own reasons for asking."

"Who? Chave Poyzner? I'll tell you everything, with pleasure," says Praeger. "She's a person who wants it all. She wants to fly in the air and to walk on the ground at the same time. She's the cause of all my sorrow. But in a manner of speaking she's not only my personal tragedy but everyone's. She's just like her father. Once she hated him but now she adores him and does whatever he asks. Every morning she cracks his eggs open for him and salts them, and she makes sure he finishes them before she leaves. It's as if she's doing penance for all her youthful sins. But I know that if the occasion ever arose she'd do it all again, only with more flair this time. Where are you going, Zalker? Just see who's knocking at the door."

Shaulke the tailor's apprentice and black-haired Leah have been in the large, empty storage room behind the door for some minutes now. Leah is wrapped in her mother's long, warm shawl and is seething with anger. The tailor's apprentice lied to her. He told her that Zalker the agent wanted her to explain why she was late with her weekly payment, but he brought her to this storage room instead. As soon as she saw the bed with the dirty mattress on it she wanted to leave, but Shaulke blocked her way.

"Where are you going?"

"Leave me alone!"

"Take it easy!"

Black-haired Leah doesn't say another word and pulls the shawl over her head, covering her face except for her nose, mouth, and eyes. Then she marches angrily across the room, trying to keep him from looking at her. The tailor's apprentice remains calm. Taking off his hat, he wipes his brow and begins to roll a cigarette.

"Oh, so you want to run away, do you. Did you run away from your student Brill, too?"

Leah is really seething now. She hears voices coming from the adjoining room and making a dash for the door that leads into it, she pounds on it with all her might. Shaulke throws down his hat and the cigarette he is rolling and grabs her by the waist.

"Get away from there!" he shouts.

"I won't."

"Come here, I say!" and the tailor's apprentice pulls her from the door and presses his body against hers. Then, his face flushed, he carries her to the bed and throws her down on the filthy mattress, jumping on top of her at the same time. Her hands are clasped as tightly as springs but he only presses down harder on her, breathing heavily.

"Oh, look at the little damp chin. Doesn't it taste good. It smells like Brill the student."

She turns her face from side to side to keep him from kissing her and then bites him hard on his left shoulder. The door from Praeger's room opens. . . .

.   .   .

Chaim Moshe is no longer there. He returned to the forest after he gave Zalker the bills of the pharmacy inventory. The walking corpse with the puny beard is back to repairing the accordion, blowing and rattling in time with the notes he plays. Praeger is lying on the hard bench, his hands under his head, thinking about the events of the long day. He talked about Chave Poyzner today, after a long period of silence on the subject and he is nervous and exhausted. The sun has set and the evening begins to fill every corner of the room at the end of this first day of the fair. Peasants are bustling about and driving home, their squealing pigs tied up in the wagons. The sound of drunken peasants dancing at a nearby wedding can be heard. Zalker, the only one left at the table with the bottles, is shouting for Shaulke and black-haired Leah to come in from the next room.

Praeger gets up from the bench, dresses, and without stopping to eat goes out to wander around the fair, aimlessly. This was the strangest fair day he has ever experienced. He walked through the market today and watched his pupils, the little Talmud Torah boys, helping their sweaty fathers sell the merchandise in the various stalls. They love him, these children of his.

"Hello, Teacher," they call out cheerfully from behind the stalls.

Now in the evening as he walks through the empty market, he sees the children again, rummaging through the colored wrapping paper and the broken boxes behind the stalls, searching, eternally searching.

XVIII

By Tuesday evening the last of the peasants have returned to their homes. Only children remain in the empty marketplace, rummaging through the discarded wrapping paper and the broken boxes. In town everyone watches as a brand-new, light-colored carriage with rubber wheels and soft springs rolls smoothly through the main street. The carriage has very deep seats that are fitted with a backrest made up of four pillows upholstered in a blue fabric. Yan, Dessler's servant, is the driver. His uniform consists of a long jacket with brass buttons and a wrinkled cap. And, like all the older coachmen, he holds a whip in his hand. The strong, spirited horses lift their heads high and whinny as they ride into the sunset.

Why does Yan drive through Rakitne so often? Is it to show the people of Rakitne that the trip from Berizshinetz is easy for these strong black horses? Or is the carriage tied in some way to Rakitne now? Everyone in the shtetl is curious.

Dessler and Chave Poyzner are in the carriage. He has on his hard brown hat and holds his head a little to the side. She is hatless, in a low-cut dress of white batiste, and smiles as her hair blows in the wind. The women who are watching from their open doors agree that she is very beautiful.

"She's like a queen."

"Thank God that she finally came to her senses and realizes that her affair with Praeger was only a childish game."

Shadows begin to fall, modestly veiling everything outside. From the distance there is a sound of thunder, signaling rain, though it might be a shooting match in the nearby summer camp. The ground smells of damp grass. The shiny new carriage with its whispering springs continues on its way down the hill, toward the old part of the shtetl. Dessler and Chave Poyzner ride through every dark and wretched alley, talking and laughing all the time. When they pass Zanvil Potshter's basement inn where Praeger the principal lives Chave Poyzner becomes even more animated and laughs louder than ever. Dessler smiles at her lovingly.

. . .

On that same evening Azriel Poyzner is called home from the store. His wife has something to tell him, they say without much enthusiasm. In that spirit he leaves.

He finds her in the dining room, rushing around and making elaborate preparations for a party, and he watches her coolly, with myopic eyes, stroking his beard toward his neck.

"Well—what is it?"

"Nothing. What should there be?"

But she nods in the direction of a room at the far end of the house. Chave and Dessler are there.

"Chave told me a short while ago that she wants to announce her engagement this evening."

"Well, well, well," he says, continuing to stroke his beard.

His wife is trying to spread a fresh white tablecloth over the table, and seeing her struggle, he takes hold of one end and pulls the two corners towards him. He has never done this before in his life. Of all times, this is the day the servant chose to visit her relatives in the old shtetl. Leyzer has been sent to find her.

Azriel Poyzner goes into the bedroom, gets his Sabbath shoes from under the bed, and stares at them. He is thinking about himself and Dessler and the engagement they will soon celebrate. Dessler is very rich, and he and Chave made the match by themselves. No one else is involved.

If he and his wife dress up it will look as if they're parvenus who come from the wrong side of the tracks. He's still lost in thought when his wife comes into the room to change.

"Eh, I was just thinking. We don't need to . . . we'll just stay as we are," he mumbles.

"Really?"

And they agree to remain in the clothes they are wearing. Just then the maid returns and they go into the dining room to help her light the large hanging lamp. The sexton of their synagogue has already arrived, a short man, almost a dwarf, with stained hands from working in the winery on weekdays. He has a talent for sniffing out events before they are announced, like a gravedigger whose sixth sense tells him that someone has died. In his hand is a list of friends who are willing to serve as witnesses and who want to come and congratulate the family, wish them *mazel tov*. Azriel Poyzner vetoes the list. The only people he agrees to invite are the cantor, the rabbi, and a poor old relative who lives in the lower shtetl. But just as the sexton is about to leave, Azriel Poyzner asks if he should invite the ritual slaughterer, too. Apparently Azriel Poyzner is less sure of himself than he lets on.

The table is festive. Candles are burning in the silver candelabra that have been placed between two bouquets of flowers and the crystal decanters filled with liquor reflect the cheerful, dancing flames.

Outside it is gray, an ordinary evening at the end of the annual fair.

Azriel Poyzner, in his everyday gaberdine, can't think of anything to talk about with Dessler the engineer. He sits at the head of the table, playing with the buttons of his jacket. Every time someone refers to him as "father of the bride" he is startled. Surely, he thinks, someone else is being addressed, someone older and more respected, someone who's been dead for years.

Chave Poyzner, in the same white batiste dress that she wore while riding through the shtetl with Dessler, sits alone on the little sofa at the side of the room. She looks bored, as if she'd been through this ceremony at least a dozen times before and can hardly wait to get it over with.

Dessler sits at the table hatless, wearing a short modern jacket with low-cut lapels and insists on speaking Russian—

so the rabbi, the ritual slaughterer, and the sexton ignore him and talk to each other in Yiddish. In their black frock coats and beards they look like identical mannequins. They even have the same awkward gestures.

When they finish their tea the three move over to the little table that is covered with a white cloth for the occasion and begin to write the wedding contract, as if all three were needed for it. Only Azriel Poyzner's old relative with the long white beard remains at the dining room table. His face is freshly scrubbed, having just come from the bathhouse, and he wears a new velvet cap and a wide belt around his old satin frock coat. He has pulled one of the candelabra toward him and leans over a large old tome, chanting earnestly. All in good time, he thinks, the world to come as well as the delicacies that will soon be served.

The men call Azriel Poyzner over and together they decide on what passages to strike out. What is the groom's father's name? they ask. They know that he lives in the nearby city and that he is the wealthiest tax collector in the area, but no one in the room has ever heard him referred to by name. They are so embarrassed that they look the other way when the sexton asks Dessler, the groom.

Just then someone in the corridor beckons Chave Poyzner to step out of the dining room and come into the kitchen. She is gone only briefly but returns shaken, her lower lip trembling with rage.

"How crude and insolent!" is all she can bring herself to say to her mother. "I wouldn't have believed anyone capable of such vulgarity."

Later, everyone in the shtetl had something to say about it.

After the betrothal contract is signed and the plate is

broken in memory of the destruction of the Temple, the Poyzner household really becomes lively. People stop in to offer their congratulations, Madam Bromberg bringing the new government rabbi's wife with her, of course. The celebration continues through most of the night and just as the guests are ready to go home someone appears at the servants' entrance and asks, "Is it true? Are Chave Poyzner and Dessler really betrothed?"

The kitchen maid refuses to identify the man, but the next morning many people claim to have seen Praeger walking near the house. Praeger pays no attention to what they say. He has fought with three-quarters of the people in the shtetl and knows how much they dislike him. If only half of their wishes were to come true, there would be nothing left of him but dust and ashes. He is no longer interested in Chaike the servant and never visits her behind the inn anymore. Let Yossl, the department store clerk, have her—and good luck to them both!

.   .   .

By the next morning it is cold and windy, but despite the bitter winter weather Praeger goes out, too restless to stay in his room. He puts on his heavy brown coat, which makes him look older than he is, and walks to the Brombergs'. All morning long he talks and talks and when he meets Chaim Moshe in the street later in the day he continues the conversation with him.

"That was quite a celebration last night, don't you agree, Chaim Moshe? Everyone I meet today looks exhausted. Something momentous has happened. Chave Poyzner is betrothed to Dessler. It's official now, *finita la commedia*. Last night the virago was betrothed to the devil," and Praeger laughs so hard that he has to hold his pince-nez to keep them from falling off his nose. "That man is inhuman," he continues. "He may be an engineer, but he's not human."

. . .

Four years ago when he first came to take over his share of the peat bogs in Ritnitz he spent two weeks walking in mud that came over his boots, he and his devoted servant Yan. He lived in one side of an apartment that he rented from a non-Jewish widow, the former wife of the station master, and used to go around in his dressing gown and slippers at home.

"Yan," he would call through the window, "I want you up here in exactly forty-seven minutes. Is that clear? Look at your watch."

And Yan would keep his eyes glued on his military watch to make sure that he was on time. That's how hard Dessler was on his servant Yan.

In the rented apartment he saw to it that the widow and her children used the two spittoons he bought in the city, instead of the floor. When brokers ran after him in the street with contracts to sign, he wouldn't even turn around, as if to say, I'll do business with you in my office, but in the street I don't even know you. And to this day he speaks to older people in the most disrespectful way, always using the familiar pronoun.

When he walks into his brewery you can hear a pin drop. The place becomes as quiet as a cemetery. Zalker the agent, who was there once, said that even the bottles shake with fear. And he doesn't trust anyone with the keys except his non-Jewish servant Yan.

One hot day during the summer Dessler saw the bookkeeper, Froyke Neches, working in his shirt-sleeves while several customers were waiting for their receipts. Dessler called the bookkeeper into his private office and dismissed him on the spot, without warning.

"Get out." he said. "Leave right now."

And while the man was still there, frozen in his place, he sent Yan to bring back another bookkeeper from the city.

"Why? Why have I been dismissed?" asked Froyke Neches, trembling.

"I don't want to hear any complaints. This is not a study house where you can sit in your shirt-sleeves."

The bookkeeper is the sole source of support of his widowed mother and younger brothers who study in Praeger's Talmud Torah.

"Oh, woe is me, my Froyke has been fired," the mother cries to anyone who will listen.

But no one can help her. Dessler turns a deaf ear to everyone. That's when Chave Poyzner stepped in. It was just at the time that she had decided to change her life and help the poor. She hired the handsomest droshky in Rakitne and drove straight to Dessler's brewery, working her magic on him in his private office. Dessler gave in and even ended the conversation with a smile. "You win. I'll take the bookkeeper back."

That's how the relationship between Chave Poyzner and Dessler began. The good deed seems to have touched a nerve in both of them that awakened their feelings for each other.

But Chaim Moshe is not listening. He is anxiously watching a small side street next to Poyzner's department store where a woman in a white dress is walking with a parasol in hand. The young woman—is it Channeke Loyber?—looks in Chaim Moshe's direction and starts to walk towards him, but changes her mind and turns back.

"I don't understand it," says Chaim Moshe. "Zalker was supposed to send two wagons from Berizshinetz to pick up Melech's inventory. They should have been here yesterday."

Then he remembers something he was supposed to take care of in Melech's pharmacy and Praeger, having nothing better to do, decides to go along.

The entire inventory is packed and ready to go. The boxes are piled one on top of the other and the glass cabinets are wrapped in burlap. Praeger remembers the pills that Melech had given him after he'd been drinking, really exceptional pills. As Chaim Moshe rummages through the papers in Melech's desk he empties everything into a box. Piles of letters, a purse, notebooks. When he finds a small, neatly wrapped package he puts it into his pants pocket. Everything is ready now and he closes the box.

"Remind Zalker that this box isn't part of the inventory," says Chaim Moshe to Praeger.

.   .   .

For the next few days Praeger stays in his room, lying on his hard bench and waiting for a miracle, or at least for someone to visit him. But no one comes except Shaulke the tailor's apprentice who is looking for Zalker, so he becomes Praeger's guest. The two spend the day together, drinking Zanvil's concoction—slowly at first until they get used to it.

Every time he is drunk Praeger gets disgusted with his life and with Rakitne. He wants to leave, go somewhere else. Lying on his hard bench, he thinks about himself and Chave Poyzner, and about various remedies that people have come up with to end their own suffering.

In his mind's eye he pictures a towel, an ordinary long towel, hanging from a hook in the ceiling. His imagination also conjures up a small package with a label showing a skull and crossbones. Where did he see a small package like that recently? Try as he would, he can't recall, not until Zalker the agent stops by. Then he is suddenly reminded of the little package that Chaim Moshe put into his pocket. He is shocked! He can't believe it.

XIX

According to Esther Fich, Chaim Moshe found some things belonging to Chave Poyzner at Melech's place and returned them to her.

"There's no point in my taking these things to Isaac Ber's house in the forest," he told her.

Soon after that Chaim Moshe was observed rushing all over town, trying to settle his affairs. It seems that he is packed and ready to leave, and the sooner the better. He even went to visit his old friend from heder days, Fishl Richtman, in the lower shtetl. He had been a student once, but now he deals in old burlap sacks, like his father-in-law.

"What do you have to say for yourself, Chaim Moshe? Did you accomplish what you came for? Did you set things right?" asks Fishl Richtman.

The two men are sitting together in the old house that he inherited. Fishl Richtman has a baby in his arms and is waiting for his wife to come home. She has gone to visit someone in the upper shtetl.

"No, I didn't accomplish a thing," says Chaim Moshe, pacing the floor nervously, and as soon as Fishl finishes giving him the latest news Chaim Moshe rushes back to his room in the forest.

.   .   .

"Are you ready, Melech?"

"I'm ready, Chaim Moshe."

"Then come, Melech, come to your reckoning."

.   .   .

Chaim Moshe is looking at the little bust of Melech on the dresser across from his bed, the bust with the bashful smile.

If Isaac Ber is silent, it isn't to imitate you, Melech. The opposite is the case. Remember, he fought with God when he was still a young man. What's the point of being gentle in a world that doesn't understand gentleness? Why do you smile, Melech?

How much fanaticism, how much stubbornness is in that goodness of yours! You never understood the world, Melech. Why did you leave so quietly? It should have been different. You should have slammed the door hard, so hard that the house shook, that the children woke up from their sleep.

Isaac Ber is old and tired. He doesn't have the strength to slam the door and he always feels the silent burden of having fought with God in his youth. Every evening, after counting the felts and arguing with his religious wife and with the young assistant whom he doesn't trust with the cashbox, he comes to my room, his arms folded in his sleeves and a melancholy expression on his face, like a mourner who has just buried God. He stands in the dark for hours at a time, leaning against the wall and waiting for a sign that he has been redeemed. It's as if he's saying, I, Isaac Ber, began the process that you, Chaim Moshe, must continue. You have a responsibility.

But what am I supposed to do?

Praeger the principal says that he has no obligation to Melech, or to anyone else. A person's only obligation is to himself.

.   .   .

Fishl Richtman has a lot to talk about.

"Praeger says that he doesn't owe anyone a thing, so if he wants to invite Zalker the agent and Shaulke the tailor's apprentice in for a drink, it's no one's business but his own. As far as he's concerned, the respectable people in town can bust a gut. Praeger also tells everyone that Chaim Moshe spent the day with him in his room. And when they ask him what sort of a person he is, he squeezes his pince-nez with his middle three fingers and says Chaim Moshe claims that he's a dissatisfied person, and that only the dissatisfied can change the world."

"Anshl Zudik, the skeptic, thinks it's all nonsense, the kind of nonsense they discuss in the marketplace. If Zalker the agent isn't happy with his wife and Shaulke the tailor's apprentice likes black Leah but can't have her, does that make the world a better place? Anshl Zudik lived in Palestine for a few years, and now he's convinced that nothing good can come out of the exile."

At this point in the conversation Fishl's wife comes back.

"See what an honored guest we have with us," says Fishl.

She is happy that Chaim Moshe is visiting them. In a flash the samovar is lit and the table is covered with a bright cloth. It looks very festive.

"Please stay for tea, Chaim Moshe. When you're with us it's a party."

Fishl's wife is no ordinary woman and it is not by accident that she chose the former student over the other young men in Rakitne. She looks a bit older than he, but her face has that special quality, a kind of glow found in people who strive to live on a higher spiritual plane. She's a quiet person, like everyone in her impoverished family, and she speaks with measured restraint, like a rabbi's wife who refuses to engage in gossip. But she has a profound understanding of human nature. She believes that nothing is ever as clear-cut and simple as it appears to be.

"There are two sides to everything, and a layer in the middle, too," she says, moving the suckling baby from one side to the other. "Take Chave Poyzner, for instance. She had to fight like a demon to catch Dessler. It couldn't have been easy to rouse an icy soul like his. And she had several affairs of her own before Dessler."

"Oyzer Loyber has reasons of his own for remaining in Kiev for months at a time. He probably lives there with a woman, and a non-Jewish woman at that. It doesn't bother him to be the subject of gossip. His mill is thriving and he'll just give more to charity. An extra thousand means nothing to him. But Channeke Loyber is cut from a different cloth. She's more like her mother. I'm related to some distant relatives of hers so I know her well. She's a very special person— there's no one like her in the world. While her father is off in the city, she stays at home with her little brother, Motik, and cares for him like a mother."

Chaim Moshe, delighted to have heard these things from Fishl Richtman's wife, says goodbye and takes his leave.

·   ·   ·

Later that week, while walking near the young poplars in the town square during the hottest hour of the day when the street is deserted, he sees Channeke. His eyes light up and her heart skips a beat and leaves her breathless. Finally she says, "Esther Fich told me that you're leaving."

"Esther Fich?"

"Yes. She told me that you're definitely leaving soon."

Now he remembers. He met Esther Fich in town one day and when she asked him when he planned to leave Rakitne he told her that it would be soon. That's all he said.

Channeke lowers her long lashes. She takes in every word Chaim Moshe says and feels all choked up as they stroll together towards her house.

"Perhaps we'd better part here," she whispers.

"Channeke, are you in a hurry to go somewhere?"

Silence. Then, without looking at him she says, "We both left home this morning for a purpose and it would have been better if we had done what we set out to do. No, I'm not in a hurry—it's just that it would have been simpler that way. I would have gone on to the next street and asked when Ethel Kadis was expected back. Then I would have gone home to Motik and nothing would have happened. But now . . ."

And feeling Chaim Moshe's hand on hers, she knows that something is happening, something very important. She has forgotten all about Motik . . .

"At first I thought that I wanted nothing from you, Chaim Moshe, nothing at all. It was enough for me to know that you were in the forest—I didn't need to see you. But every time there was a knock on the door I hoped it was you. I couldn't stop thinking about you, I wanted to see you so much. Once, when I came out of Poyzner's department store I saw you and Praeger standing in the street, talking. I must have looked like a fool as I started to walk towards you, then quickly pulled back. Twice I did the same thing. I'm ashamed to talk like this. I even wrote a poem that day, the first poem I ever wrote. Something foolish that I tore up the next day. It was only because I was so anxious to see you. I've always been afraid of wanting something very much. Perhaps I'm religious, like my mother. She died when Motik was an infant. My older brother, who was still living at home then, took some money from the cashbox and ran away. That was when I decided that I must never want anything very much. It would be a crime and I must never permit it to happen. But then why do I always think that it's even harder for you, Chaim Moshe, that everything is much, much harder for you? I don't pretend to know what's best for you or where it's best for you to be. Esther Fich the student only adds to my confusion. 'You'll see soon enough,' she says to me every time she visits. 'I only hope that I'm wrong.'"

Again Channeke chokes up and again Chaim Moshe tries to comfort her.

"It's not harder for me," he says, "really it's not. At times I actually feel guilty about it. Think of Isaac Ber, for instance. Do you know him? His life is worse, much, much worse than mine. I spent the summer in Rakitne, becoming reacquainted with my home town. But now that the inventory is sold I'm just waiting for Zalker the agent to pick it up so that I can send the money to Melech's mother. I come every day to see if the wagons have arrived yet. Today I went to your house, Channeke—I wanted to see you. When I'm in the forest I think about you so often, and now I'm here, holding your hand and looking into your eyes. What if Melech were still alive and we went to visit him together? Would you want to see Melech now, Channeke? Why are you suddenly so pale? Why do you close your eyes, as if you're about to say a silent prayer? Oh, Channeke, if this conversation upsets you I'll stop right now. Come, I'll take you home. I want to go back to the forest. There's something I have to do, some unfinished business to attend to.

Upset, he returns to his room in the forest to think things through, but the phrase "What if Melech?" repeats itself over and over again in his mind and keeps him from concentrating.

Finally he sits down at his desk and stares at the unfilled writing sheets.

.   .   .

"It doesn't make any sense to long for someone who's dead."

"The dead are reborn, Chaim Moshe."

The sun is setting and silent shadows from the forest slide through the window and slowly fill the room. Little by little, the statue of Melech darkens and the smile begins to fade. Again Chaim Moshe's work is interrupted. A door squeaks in the nearby corridor and then his own door opens.

"Who is it?"

"It's nobody, Chaim Moshe—only me, Isaac Ber.

XX

Zalker's wagons finally come from Berizshinetz and the sluggish movers spend most of the day loading them. The horses wait patiently with their harnesses loosened, chomping contentedly on their oats. When they stop to lift their heads they are startled by the unfamiliar surroundings.

By two in the afternoon the wagons are rattling noisily down the main road of Rakitne, carrying Melech's chests and boxes. His bed and some benches are tied on the top with their legs reaching towards the sky, weaving from side to side as they leave Rakitne.

Nothing is left in the shop except the bare, stained walls and a lot of torn papers strewn over the floor. Even the lock has been taken off the door. Chaim Moshe is never seen in the shtetl these days.

The Talmud Torah charity ball is fast approaching and people prepare for it as though they're going to a big, fancy wedding.

On the great day itself everyone eats lunch early. The women scrub and polish the children and the men find it difficult to concentrate on their work. A warm breeze blows the clouds to the ends of heaven, and with it the fear of rain. The warehouse in the alley near the Brombergs' patio, rented for the occasion, has been freshly whitewashed and colorfully decorated. Channeke Loyber and Esther Fich are there already, setting the tables before they go home to get dressed.

Everyone is excited about the entertainment that has been planned. Madam Bromberg has hired two bands, one local and the other from Berizshinetz, and there are to be two special performances, aside from the usual pageant and recitations by the Talmud Torah children. Anshl Zudik has prepared a parody of a long-winded preacher—and a gymnast, who is being paid well, is to play the fiddle while accompanying himself on the piano. He is coming from out of town, together with his sister and her wealthy groom. When Oyzer Loyber appears in the shtetl at three o'clock in the afternoon, everyone is delighted. He always brings in more money for this charity than anyone else.

"Well, well, well. He didn't forget us after all."

Just as the last minute preparations are being made there

is a loud roll of drums coming from the Brombergs' court-yard. The two bands are playing a lively march and the hot wind that has been blowing the clouds away and raising the dust in the main street blows the music of the marching band far, far away. Groups of barefoot girls and boys have already come from the greener, non-Jewish end of town. A barefoot nursemaid, starved for fun and the sound of lively music, is dancing a kind of jig while bouncing a baby up and down. The band is calling latecomers to hurry. Some are still comb-ing their hair or adjusting their bodices. The naked shoulders of a young woman can be seen through an open door and a hand is seen pinching a little boy who is misbehaving. The only person on the main street is the new rabbi's pug-nosed wife. In her rush to get to the warehouse early to arrange the buffet she has over-powdered her face and over-oiled her hair.

The audience is beginning to assemble in the warehouse, black and white figures walking back and forth across the cool hall. But it isn't crowded yet—the warehouse is very large.

A few young women are practicing a waltz, which the band is playing just for them. And when they suddenly stop and stand in place with sheepish grins on their faces, no one pays any attention to them. An expansive person in a heavy black suit and over-starched collar is walking with Praeger the principal across the dance floor. He is hoarse from shout-ing as he tries to round up all the Talmud Torah boys and get them to stay in the far corner of the hall, behind the curtain.

As the warehouse fills up, the air becomes heavy. And it is noisy—everyone seems to be shouting. Someone climbs up to the roof and the agile servant boy who is sent to get him down can hardly push his way out of the gate because of the press of the crowd. Isaac Ber's sickly wife is at the very back of the hall and every time she attempts to come forward she is pushed even further back.

"Please," she cries out helplessly, "I'll be trampled to death."

She is dressed in her Sabbath finery and her new silk kerchief and carries the few coins she has saved to donate to the Talmud Torah fund wrapped in a handkerchief. Shaulke the tailor's apprentice is moving tables and benches but stops when he sees her and comes to her aid.

"Let us through!" he shouts. "It's Isaac Ber's wife."

He takes her by the hand and pulls her through the crowd as if she were a child, stepping on a lot of peasant girls' bare toes on the way. All at once the bands strike up a fast polka in honor of Madam Bromberg, the main mover of the annual event. It was Dr. Grabay's idea. When the dance is over they all clap and sit down at the long, white-covered tables near the wall, ready to drink tea.

Channeke Loyber, wearing an embroidered white dress and long white gloves, is standing at the buffet near the new government rabbi's wife. Her father came home just ten minutes before she was due to be here and she is still trying to pull herself together. Motik is with him. She holds her head, trying to remember how much to charge for the various items of food, when she spots Chaim Moshe in his short gray jacket. His eyes wander around the hall, looking for someone.

"Channeke, Channeke, let me come through!" someone shouts, and she moves over as two men bring in Madam Bromberg's huge railroad station–size samovar filled with boiling water. From her new position Channeke can see Chave Poyzner, wearing a tight black décolleté dress and high-heeled shoes, standing next to Chaim Moshe. For a moment Channeke's eyes meet his, but she lowers them immediately to attend to a little girl who is helping herself to sweets from the buffet and messing up the table. Suddenly Channeke feels that her corset is too tight and pressing on her heart.

When she looks up again she sees Chave Poyzner sitting with Chaim Moshe on the red velvet sofa in the corner of the room. He looks steadily in the direction of the buffet but smiles as he listens to Chave Poyzner.

.   .   .

Just like at a wedding, everyone wants special treatment. Esther Fich has already been involved in a fracas with some women who came up to the samovar to get tea. She asked them to sit down and wait to be served at the table, but the women insisted that they'd waited long enough. They paid their entrance fees just like everyone else and they didn't want to wait while friends and family were served first. Esther Fich told them that they had no manners and if they wanted their money back they could get it and go home right now. The women were insulted and started to shout at her, and Esther Fich shot back that they could burst wide open and she still wouldn't serve them tea. It wasn't until some of the other guests intervened that they finally stopped arguing.

During the quarrel the musicians stopped playing. Everyone stood in place, feeling uncomfortable and when the band starts up again they try to forget what happened, but can't.

The two distinguished guests at the head table, Oyzer Loyber and young Bromberg, are the richest men in Rakitne. They wear elegant long black coats and have shiny skin, as though they spend hours scrubbing themselves. Both are honored and respected by everyone in town, yet they seem to be deliberately ignoring each other. Young Bromberg, in an effort to be polite, closes his nearsighted eyes, and tries to recall what he said on the same evening last year. Finally, swaying back and forth, he blurts out, "What's true is true. Praeger the principal has certainly turned the Talmud Torah into a respected institution."

But Oyzer Loyber, who doesn't think much of young Bromberg, continues to tap his fingers on the table as if he's bored and doesn't even bother to look up. He is certainly the liveliest and most spirited of all the fathers here, and the golden pince-nez he wears so proudly on his rather large nose and the strong odor of expensive soap and eau de cologne testify to his recent arrival from the home of his non-Jewish inamorata. All in all, he has the smug, self-satisfied expression of a person who is prepared to shout out, "Believe me one and all, there is nothing sweeter than having a large mill, a charming house, and a name known throughout the district."

Doctor Grabay, walking past the table, looks as if he's going to talk to Chave Poyzner and Chaim Moshe, but he doesn't sit down with them. He is on his way to the buffet to tell them to close the window—it is directly opposite the door and creates a draft. All of his patients are here and he doesn't want to hear any of them complaining of a cold. He has no patience for it.

"Hey there," he shouts, "close it fast! Get a move on!"

When he gets back to his seat the third bell has already rung and people are sitting on the benches watching the play. It opens with some boys walking back and forth on the stage, lost in the woods and frightened. Then, just as two boys step forward and announce that they will walk in another direction to try to find the way, everyone in the audience turns to the back. Dessler has arrived, they whisper, Dessler from Berizshinetz.

Madam Bromberg goes over to greet him, and the children become distracted and briefly forget their lines. They soon regain control, but the audience has become restless and talks throughout the performance. Nobody has much respect for Dessler yet they all stand up to catch a glimpse of him. At the back of the hall the gymnast from out of town, his sister, and her husband-to-be keep up a constant stage whisper. They are furious because they feel they've been slighted and are ready to go home right now, before the show even begins. Channeke is sent to talk to them.

"We'll give you a place at the head table where you'll be happy, I promise," she says tearfully before returning to the buffet.

All at once there's an even louder murmuring in the audience. Channeke is not well. She has fainted behind the buffet, in the curtained-off corner where the dishes are kept and the cakes and pastries sliced. Oyzer Loyber rushes over and finds her sitting up and sipping water already, surrounded by a small crowd. There is nothing wrong, she insists, and no, she does not want to go home with her father yet. By the time they return to the benches the play is over and the tables are being moved to the side of the hall to let Shaulke the tailor's apprentice sprinkle the floor with water from a kettle to settle the dust. People stand around in a big circle, wondering what the next event will be.

The bands strike up a tune.

. . .

By one in the morning someone has fallen asleep on a bench in the corner of the warehouse while others doze in their seats, their heads bobbing up and down uncontrollably. When they wake up they are startled by the eery sight of the three hanging lamps enveloped in mist, or is it dust? The musicians are tired, too, and play as if they're in a trance. They've put away the cymbals and without them the drums sound uninspired and monotonous. Nevertheless, the people on the floor continue their frenzied dancing. They stop only when the drums roll to a halt, a sign to rest before kicking up their heels again.

Dessler turns in his donation in a perfumed envelope and leaves for home, and when Oyzer Loyber and the younger Bromberg follow suit the young people feel less restrained and things become even livelier. The gymnast has taught them how to spin wildly in a circle of ten and to keep smiling even though they are dizzy and breathless, and then to begin all over again.

"Oh, I'm suffocating."

"Then leave."

Esther Fich, who has weak lungs, was told to get some fresh air several times by Doctor Grabay, but she doesn't listen and remains at the table with him and Chaim Moshe.

"No, I want to stay right here, and don't you or Chaim Moshe go home either, at least not until daybreak. Last year, when Melech was here, a certain someone and I refused to let him leave before morning. Now that certain someone has moved on to the second part of the plan," says Esther Fich, breaking into laughter and staring at Chave Poyzner, who is sitting alone on the satin sofa in a corner of the warehouse, looking bewildered.

That evening Praeger the principal again shows how malicious he can be by directing a few of his choice, well-aimed barbs at Chave Poyzner. After that, the evening is finished for her. She just sits, flushed and angry, unable even to carry on a conversation.

Before the unfortunate incident with Praeger she had been enjoying herself, talking to people here and there and discussing today's young people and their tasteless and vulgar behavior with Doctor Grabay.

"Just look at how they throw their bodies around on the dance floor. It's obscene, and they look so ugly."

In her opinion, everything about them is disgusting. She never took them seriously before. Once, when two of them came to her house while she was still in bed, she let them come right into her room. That's how seriously she took them.

Chave Poyzner also made an effort to talk to Chaim Moshe.

"Isaac Ber must be an interesting person, but he's such a loner and so suspicious of everyone that it's hard to talk to him," at which Chaim Moshe smiles, as if he is suspicious and untrusting, too.

Now she sits by herself on the small velvet sofa, waiting for dawn to break. Can it be that no one will offer to take her home? And while she watches the young people raising the dust, she has the feeling that over there, in the corner behind the curtain where the dishes and the cakes are kept, they are talking about her. Yes, she's sure that something is going on in that dark corner.

And she is right. After Shaulke the tailor's apprentice was paid for waiting on the tables, he stayed on to drain the last drops of liquor from the bottles stored behind the curtain.

Praeger joined him, and Anshl Zudik, and Esther Fich, who is laughing uncontrollably in her high-pitched, nasal voice. She wants to show that she can drink as much as any man. Praeger tries to monopolize the conversation by talking about every decent person in town, but Anshl Zudik is not interested in Praeger's stories. He is in his cups and thinks he's quite amazing himself.

"Chave Poyzner is a crab!" shouts Praeger, pointing to the velvet couch. "I swear to you, she's a crab!"

And in this drunken state, with his glass in his hand, he walks from one person to another, whispering in their ears and grinning as if he is being tickled. Suddenly he thinks of something that seems to him very brilliant. There's a period in a crab's life when it loses its claws and shell. At that time, with no means of causing pain, it crawls into a hole and waits patiently until the bad time comes to an end, just like Chave Poyzner right now.

But no one wants to hear his brilliant idea, and without realizing that he has already shared his great discovery with Chaim Moshe, he goes over to him again.

"Just look at her," he says, pleased with himself.

Chaim Moshe listens indifferently. Indeed, he seems to be indifferent to everything this evening as his eyes wander around the room, looking for someone. Finally he leaves the warehouse and waits near the open gate for daylight to break. From where he stands he can hear the music and see the bright lamps. Not far away, very orderly, very secure, is Bromberg's house with its neat red trim and row after row of agricultural machinery. It is strange how quickly the slow-moving, near-sighted, heavyset Bromberg was able to establish himself here, thinks Chaim Moshe. But it's none of my business, after all.

Perhaps it's all for the best that he didn't go over to Channeke Loyber. He knew all along that it would be impossible to sleep the night before his special mission. Now the sky is gray. The night is coming to an end and it will soon be daylight. There is nothing more for him to do here. He goes back into the warehouse with the mist-enveloped lamps, but there is really no need for Chaim Moshe to say goodby to anyone inside. He may as well go.

.   .   .

In that gray hour between night and day he is the only person on the dewy-wet country road outside the shtetl. As he walks, his steps slow and measured, the same thought goes through his mind over and over again: One never sleeps on the night before bringing a special undertaking to a close.

A year ago Melech spent the night the same way and when he left in the morning he was calm and smiling bashfully, as usual. Melech did things differently. He slept the night before he left us. And he never stopped smiling, not to the very end. If one is silent, then nobody is astonished at a "silent protest." Chaim Moshe has often thought about it.

.   .   .

"Why did you go so silently, Melech?"

"You know why, Chaim Moshe."

"In order not to wake up the little children?"

"Yes, Chaim Moshe, let the children sleep, let the little pale ones sleep."

"But it's nothing less than demonic to do the thing while being good and smiling bashfully."

. . .

He climbs over the forest gate and walks up to the door of Isaac Ber's sleepy house, which seems to be waiting quietly for him. The door is unlocked. It's very touching the way Isaac Ber always takes care of him. Last night, for instance, he closed the shutters in Chaim Moshe's room from the outside and didn't bolt the door on the inside so that he wouldn't have to knock.

Chaim Moshe goes quietly into his room and closes the door behind him. By the time he realizes that he's forgotten to open the shutters, he's too tired to go out again. The early morning light shines through the cracks, forming a pattern of stripes in the room. He lies awake on the bed for a very long time, staring up at the ceiling.

What is there left for me to do?

To bang my head against the wall and wait for redemption like Isaac Ber, or to give in to the feeling that drew me to Channeke all night and take her with me to the big city, where she will sit behind the curtain and listen to me teach nice boys and girls mathematics in a Talmud chant.

But there is another solution, another way. Ah, yes, how strange—of course, I remember. . . .

Looking through the papers in Melech's drawer he found a small packet with a black skull and crossbones on the tag. He put it in his pants pocket at the time, but now he can't remember what he did with it. For the life of him he can't remember what he did with it.

And suddenly, in a fit of anxiety, he pulls his suitcase out of the closet and rummages through it. And just as suddenly he stops, puts his ear to one of the cracks in the shutter and listens.

. . .

Someone is knocking very softly and hesitantly, stops, listens for a while, and then taps timidly and apprehensively again. Slowly he walks to the window on tiptoe, as if he is afraid of waking someone, and pushes the shutter open. It is broad daylight now. Far away, above the tall trees in the distance, the sun is rising—and in front of him, behind the window wet with dew, a pale and frightened young woman in a white dress and long white gloves stares straight ahead, unable to utter a sound.

"Oh, Channeke."

Bibliography

David Bergelson in English Translation

At the Depot." Translated by Ruth Wisse. In *"A Shtetl" and Other Yiddish Novellas.* New York: Behrman House, 1973

"Civil War." Translated by Seth L. Wolitz. In *Ashes Out of Hope,* edited by Irving Howe and Eliezer Greenberg. New York: Schocken, 1977.

"The Hole Through Which Life Slips." Translated by Reuben Bercovitch. In *Ashes Out of Hope,* edited by Irving Howe and Eliezer Greenberg. New York: Schocken, 1977.

"In a Backwoods Town." Translated by Bernard Guilbert Guerney. In *A Treasury of Yiddish Stories,* edited by Irving Howe and Eliezer Greenberg. New York: Viking, 1953.

"Joseph Schur." Translated by Leonard Wolf. In *Ashes Out of Hope,* edited by Irving Howe and Eliezer Greenberg. New York: Schocken, 1977.

When All Is Said and Done. Translated by Bernard Martin. Athens: Ohio Univ. Press, 1977.

Books Consulted

Brianski, S. *David Bergelson in the Mirror of Criticism, 1909–1932* (in Yiddish). Kiev, 1934.

Dobrushin, Y. *David Bergelson* (in Yiddish). Moscow, 1947.

Glatstein, Jacob. *Literary Essays* (in Yiddish). New York: F. Glatshteyn, 1978.

Howe, Irving, and Eliezer Greenberg, eds. *Ashes Out of Hope.* New York: Schocken, 1977.

—————. *A Treasury of Yiddish Stories.* New York: Viking, 1953.

Levin, Nora. *The Jews in the Soviet Union since 1917.* New York: New York Univ. Press, 1988.

Liptzin, Sol. *The Flowering of Yiddish Literature.* New York: Yoseloff, 1965.

—————. *The History of Yiddish Literature.* New York: Jonathan David, 1972.

—————. *The Maturing of Yiddish Literature.* New York: Yoseloff, 1970.

Madison, Charles. *Yiddish Literature.* New York: Ungar, 1968.

Meisel, Nahman. *Beginnings: David Bergelson* (in Yiddish). Kibbutz Alonim, 1977.

Miron, Dan. *A Traveler Disguised.* New York: Schocken, 1973.

Nowersztern, Abraham. "One Hundred Years of David Bergelson: Materials for His Life and His Work" (in Yiddish). *Die goldene keit* (Tel Aviv) 115, 1985.

—————. "Structural Aspects of David Bergelson's Prose from Its Beginnings until 'Mides-Hadin'" (in Hebrew). Ph.D. diss., Hebrew Univ., Jerusalem, 1981.

Rapoport, Louis. *Stalin's War Against the Jews: The Doctor's Plot and the Soviet Solution.* New York: Free Press, 1990.

Raskin, Aaron. *Essays in Literary Criticism* (in Yiddish). Jerusalem: I. L. Peretz, 1989.

Roback, A. A. *The Story of Yiddish Literature.* New York: YIVO, 1940.

Roskies, David. *Against the Apocalypse.* Cambridge, Mass.: Harvard Univ. Press, 1984.

Shmeruk, Khone, ed. *A Mirror on a Stone* (in Yiddish). Jerusalem: Magnes, 1988.

Slotnick, Susan Ann. "The Novel Form in the Works of David Bergelson." Ph.D. diss., Columbia Univ., 1978.

Swayze, Harold. *Political Control of Literature in the USSR, 1946–1959*. Cambridge, Mass.: Harvard Univ. Press, 1962.

Wiener, Leo. *The History of Yiddish Literature in the Nineteenth Century*. New York: Scribner's, 1899.

Wisse, Ruth, ed. *A Shtetl and Other Yiddish Novellas*. New York: Behrman, 1973.